THE IRON AGE

Arja Kajermo

illustrated by

Susanna Kajermo Törner

THE IRON AGE

First published 2017 by
Tramp Press
www.tramppress.com

All characters in this publication are fictitious, and any resemblances to real persons, living or dead, are purely coincidental.

A shorter version of *The Iron Age* was shortlisted for the 2014 Davy Byrnes Short Story Award and published in *Davy Byrnes Stories 2014* (Stinging Fly Press).

A CIP record for this title is available from the British library.

10 9 8 7 6 5 4 3 2 1

Tramp Press gratefully acknowledges the financial assistance of the Arts Council.

ISBN 978-0-9934592-3-8

Thank you for supporting independent publishing.

Set in 11 pt on 16.5 pt Minion by Marsha Swan.
Printed by Scandbook in Sweden.

To Terho and Tuomo

Part One

1

IT WAS FINLAND, it was the 1950s but on our farm it could have been the Iron Age. We had a horse to take us places, the dirt track allowed no cars near us. I was four and had never seen a car, but I had seen a picture of one. We had heard of electricity but we didn't have it. Time moved slowly then and things did not change much. The winters were colder and the summers were hotter.

One such hot day Grandmother took me with her to visit her niece Miina. My hair was plaited tight till it hurt. My eyes were pulled into slits. If I had dared I would have sobbed. The boots hurt too. They were hand-me-downs from my older brother, made for him by Mother's father, who was a shoemaker.

Grandmother moved uphill along the dirt road at a steady pace like a Russian tank. It was hard to keep up.

The dirt road was only wide enough for a horse and cart but the trees around it had been cut down to the width of a boulevard in Helsinki. Miina's husband Aleksis had cut the fir trees down when Miina had started crying, shortly after their wedding. She had cried for weeks until people started talking. Word got around. When word gets around, help is on the way. That was the way it was in our parish.

Married men came to give advice to Aleksis. They told him what all married men knew. Women get depressed if the pine trees grow too close to the house. Pine trees are dark trees and their ominous rustling brings on sadness in women. Aleksis cleared an area the size of several fields around the house. Still Miina cried. She wouldn't stop.

The married men came back. It was true that Aleksis had cut a lot of trees and the timber would pay for a whole season's fertilizer, which was good. But he would have to do better, for women can be hard to please. Cut more, said the men, come on now, give her a view.

So Aleksis cut a wide path along the dirt road so that Miina could see all the way to Grandmother's farm from her kitchen window. She stopped crying then. And Aleksis bought fertilizer for the money he got for the timber. And also a few metres of nice blue fabric with a flower pattern for a new dress, and a few metres of chequered cotton for a new pinafore for Miina. Quite a few metres, because Miina had got stout from lying in bed crying.

Miina enjoyed visitors. She clapped her hands with pleasure when people entered her house. And we had brought her a cake made with five big hen eggs.

Eggs were hard to come by, for we had no hens. We had rowed across the lake to the rich relatives and mentioned our lack of eggs and the farmer had offered us a good laying hen. Just take one, he said. So Grandmother had taken me outside and pointed at a hen and said catch that one. And I had spent the afternoon chasing the hen until we were both exhausted and Grandmother was in a rage. A boy had to be got to catch the hen and put it in a sack for us.

We rowed home all pleased, but the hen would not lay. The blasted creature seemed to change its nature. It grew a cocks-comb and spurs and became vicious. We had to chase it away into the forest for the fox to eat.

'I would not eat a dirty bird like that,' Grandmother said, 'they feed from the dung heap.' She was a very fastidious woman. When I once put my handkerchief on the table she flicked it down with the back of her hand with a sharp intake of breath and such a look of disgust on her face that the shame burnt in my cheeks for years thinking about it.

After getting rid of the hen that really was a cock we rowed to the other end of the lake and told the other rich relatives about the bad hen we had been given, and how we had no eggs. And they sent a child to find half a dozen eggs for us. Really good eggs they were and we returned to thank them when they were all gone. We never rowed home from their farm without our half dozen eggs. When the eggs were gone we rowed back for more under some pretext or other.

'To be the poor relation of rich people is good in some ways and bad in other ways,' said Grandmother, pulling hard at the oars.

Now five of the latest batch of eggs had gone into the cake that Grandmother had baked for Miina. We stepped quietly into the house because we had manners. People from the town bang on doors and shout greetings when entering, startling people who may be having a midday nap. We sat down on the bench nearest to the door and waited for Miina to ask us to move forward. We sat a long time waiting. My eyes wandered around the room. Everything was the same as on our farm. Three windows, one at the back and one to the front and one at the gable wall and a stone oven that took up nearly one quarter of the room and the benches secured to the walls and the big table in the middle and the trestle bed at the far wall. The house was so new that the timbers were still white and smelling of fresh wood, not dark brown with age like the timbers in our house. Grandmother hissed at me not to be staring at everything mouth agape like a beggar's child. Grandmother had grown up on a wealthy farm and had manners that she always tried to teach me. I lowered my gaze and folded my hands into my pinafore. Grandmother was staring straight ahead at Miina who was sitting in her rocking chair asleep. I could tell from Grandmother's face that she did not like what she saw.

Miina was napping in her rocking chair oblivious to our presence. When she finally began to wake and became aware of us her big face lit up and she clapped her hands with pleasure.

Grandmother made the usual formal apology: 'Here we are, God help us, disturbing good hardworking people …'

'So you are!' said Miina with feeling. And then her chin fell towards her bosom and her eyes closed. The rocking chair continued to rock. A light snoring buzz surrounded the scene.

Miina had fallen asleep again.

IT WAS A HABIT Miina had. She fell asleep at odd times. She had fallen asleep when she was getting married and had to be shaken and shouted at to be woken for the 'I do'. She fell asleep in the sauna. She fell asleep making hay. She fell asleep milking. And she fell asleep when visitors came.

Grandmother and I looked at each other. Had Miina really told us so rudely that we were unwelcome? Surely not. We watched while Miina slept and listened to the sound of bluebottles and Miina's snoring. Time seemed to stand still.

In the end we stood up to leave. Grandmother hesitated, but then she took the cake. It would have been wrong to leave Miina a reminder of our visit and her embarrassing lapse.

WE WALKED BACK DOWN the hill all subdued and full of thoughts. Grandmother sighed heavily and muttered to herself. She said that Miina should keep her eyes open more. Aleksis had been wandering, she said, he had been seen with a married woman behind a barn and more than once too. There had been tracks in the snow and in the muck. His boots and smaller boots. He had been seen where he should not have been seen. And sometimes it was hard to blame him – what with Miina letting herself go like that.

Not that Aleksis would get away with anything, the little scut! Next time he was seen out and about at dusk where he had no business being stern measures would be taken.

He would do well to consider what happened to his dog Nalle who had turned out bad and had to be shot in the end, which was a shame for such a promising dog.

But that is another story.

2

LET ME TELL YOU THE STORY of Nalle and Nille. They were both fine dogs of a breed called Finnish spitz. They are hunting dogs and very economical in their whelping. There are usually no more than four in a litter.

When four pups were born to the good hunting bitch at Moor House Farm the pups were carefully placed with relatives. The strongest was earmarked for Miina who was a daughter of the farm. Or Miina's Aleksis rather, for what use is a dog to a woman? The second and third were also promising-looking and went to a strong farmer nearby. Father got the fourth. Father's great-uncle pushed the pup forward with the toe of his boot.

'That one is for you,' he said.

Aleksis's pup looked like a bear so it was given a bear's name – Nalle. Ours was named Nille because it rhymes with Nalle. It was a name with no meaning but it is good to rhyme names. There is comfort and continuity in rhyming. Nalle-Nille-Kille-Kalle. Or Marja-Tarja-Arja-Irja. Endless possibilities.

Father was a bit miffed about getting the runt. But he was glad to have a dog because he was a keen hunter and a good shot. When his grey eyes fastened on a bird his rifle would go to his shoulder and the bird would drop from the sky. He seldom missed because he had practised on Russians for four years at the front.

But Aleksis was a few years younger and had not been in the war. He could not hit a bottle on a tree stump, damn it. It was unfair that he should have Nalle, the better dog.

Anyway, Nille was coming on. She was a natural. She did not need telling, she knew what to do. She turned her grey puppy coat into the red adult coat of the spitz. Her tail curled over her back, her ears were pricked, she looked alert.

Apart from her legs being on the short side she looked unusually pure-bred for a village dog. She was the real thing. The pitch-black nose twitched, she was ready to go.

And when she ran into the forest it was not long before machine-gun bursts of barking were heard. Ra-ra-ra-rah! Ra-ra–ra-rah-rah-rah! She had found a capercaillie and she had chased it up a tree. The bird sat high up in the tree watching the barking dog. Nille's tail spun like a propeller, making the bird dizzy. Nille knew to bark from the other side of the tree so that when Father caught up he could take aim and shoot the bird in the back.

And Father carried the large bird home and threw it proudly on the floor for Mother to deal with. It is said of the capercaillie that it tastes of turpentine because of its diet of pinecones. But we had a diet of potatoes and gruel, and pinecone-flavoured meat was a welcome change.

Mother set to without delay and by the evening we had a huge stew. Such happiness! And what pride we took in our fine loyal hound, Nille.

Nalle on the other hand …

Nalle did not live up to expectations. To begin with, his coat did not turn the right red colour. He had black marks along the sides. One of his ears hung at a jaunty angle instead of being pricked up like the ears of a Finnish spitz should be.

There was something of the hare-hound about him, the men said. Would he be good for hunting hares or would he go for the capercaillie, they mused.

It turned out he was good for neither.

Nalle was pursuing his own agenda. He kept running away. Like all dogs, he spent most of the day chained in the yard to keep watch. But the minute he was released he disappeared into the undergrowth and next he would be seen in another parish making a nuisance of himself. When he was brought home on a chain he was sullen and uncooperative.

During one runaway episode he was seen chasing ewes. This meant Nalle was for the bullet. Aleksis had to put his rifle into Nalle's ear and pull the trigger.

'A distance from which it is hard to miss,' the men muttered. And took deep pulls on their cigarettes and coughed.

After this we were extra pleased with our Nille. The runt had turned into one of Father's triumphs.

And there were not many of those.

3

'ELEVEN YEARS AGO on this day Risto was fatally wounded …'

Every morning, Mother and Father got up at four if it was summer and five if it was winter. If I woke I would stay in my bed in the main room and listen to their quiet murmuring as they spoke companionably over breakfast in the kitchen. Every day was an anniversary of someone's death. Some had died in their beds from a fever or a weak heart or old age, but most had fallen in the war. They never mentioned birthdays.

After all, a child has achieved nothing except being born and any fool could do that. A godmother would send her godchild a card when the child's name-day came up in the calendar. But a birthday? Better wait and see if you amounted to anything by the time you died; whether you were worth mentioning at all, or best forgotten.

Then Mother and Father would discuss what they had dreamt in the night. There were secret clues in these dreams and omens for the future. Or warnings about people who seemed like your friends but were secretly ill-disposed toward you. Sometimes the dead came back with messages. The meaning of a dream was a riddle that could be hard to tease out.

'He was coming up from the lake and stopped by the rowan tree and gave me a strange smile ... Then he turned back without saying anything ... What do you think it means?'

'A smile is a good thing?' Mother was always looking for good signs. But Father was cautious and slow to be reassured.

'It was more of a sarcastic smile.'

Then it was time for them to go out and see to the cattle and Mother had to get the cows milked. I went back to sleep.

When they came back in for their 'second breakfast' the day started for real and things got tense. Father barked orders.

'Up! Out! And about!'

That meant Tapio and Tuomas, who were seven and eight, had to get up, get ready and start walking the five kilometres to school.

It was a long walk for small boys with short legs. Sometimes Father's uncle on the next farm would give them and our cousin Hilma a loan of a horse to take them. The horse had been conscripted for two wars and had survived and was so biddable that the children could turn him around when they got to school and tell him to go back home. And the horse went straight back on his own. Unless it heard an aeroplane above. Then, it would run in under a pine tree, cart and all, and tremble violently. Luckily there were few aeroplanes about.

In the winter the boys got on their skis. In those days, the weather was never too cold, the snow was never too deep nor a storm too fierce to go to school.

Mother filled bottles of milk and put them in their rucksacks. Grandmother told them to call in to farmhouses on the way and warm themselves up a little if they felt frostbite setting in.

'The old woman is getting soft,' Father laughed (sarcastically). 'She did not worry about me on my way to school. And the weather was worse then!'

So Tapio and Tuomas set off on their skis. If there was a hard frost and a good crust on top of the snow they were in school in no time. They would arrive ruddy-cheeked and ready for their lessons in humiliation and multiplication, and the names of Jacob's twelve sons and so forth.

But the weather could change and on the way home a storm could be blowing and they would struggle against the wind. The snow was all wrong and the skis would not glide well. Then they had to stop at a farmhouse halfway and the farmer's wife would say 'poor mites' and rub their hands with snow to prevent frostbite. This would make their hands swell up even worse and the pain made them cry. And the storm was so hard that it blew them backwards on their skis. And then Tapio broke the point of his ski. So they had to walk carrying their skis through the snow that was up to their waists, and knowing that the broken point would not please Father who would laugh bitterly and say 'Again! How many points have you broken this winter? Damn it!'

But what did they know about hardship? Everything had been worse when Father was a boy. His father, who was our dead Grandfather, day of death carefully noted, had been a strict parent. When it was minus-thirty degrees, Father would tell Tapio and Tuomas 'It could be minus-forty in my day and still there was no escape from school then. I am not rearing soft boys!'

No, Father had never had it soft. He joined the Civil Guard, a voluntary right-wing defence corps, as soon as he was out of short trousers. All the lads in the parish joined, those lads who came from people with land or privilege, no matter how little. The others were not welcome. Why train people in the use of arms if they had nothing to defend?

With a bit of luck Father could have been in the Winter War in 1939. It was a short and glorious war and the officers died all the time and a smart lad from the Civil Guard could have been promoted in that war, Father said. He could have come home in glory with stripes on his shoulders. Instead, he had to wait for the next war, the Continuation War. He signed on for that one before he was called up, he couldn't wait. But it was not as glorious as he had been led to believe. And it dragged on and on for four years. And the officers did not fall at the rate he had hoped for, so he was never promoted. And the defeat was even worse than in the previous war. All he came home with was a handful of medals, same as everyone. And a few bits of shrapnel in his legs.

Somehow he blamed Grandmother for this. He had not been let go to join the war when the time was right for him.

Because he was too young then. Because he did not have the right birthday and whose fault was that?

Father shot a black look at Grandmother.

4

GRANDMOTHER WAS AN ANGRY WOMAN. She was angry with Father most days. When he wanted to buy tools she said new tools is it now? What next? And where would the money for that come from? And he could forget about her signing over the farm to him. Over her dead body would he get the farm. As long as she was walking and breathing, the farm was hers.

But most of all she was angry with Grandfather because he was dead. She had been angry with him while he was alive too. So many reasons. Where to begin? All Grandfather could do was smoke and talk. And what use is that if you don't have a big farm to back up your opinions.

Grandfather had been one of many younger sons from a big farm. When he got his inheritance he went to St Petersburg and bought a gold fob watch for himself and a Swiss wristwatch for Grandmother. Grandmother was a pretty girl from a wealthy farm and a good catch. She was mesmerised by the watch and grandfather was a dapper little man who had been to agricultural college.

So they got married, worse luck, and Grandmother was the sorry woman and the babies kept coming. Father was the first-born. A son! But Grandmother did not like the look of him. When his dark slate grey eyes turned a pale shade of grey, she liked him less.

After a few years living with Grandmother on his folk's land, Grandfather was given his own farm. It was a smallholding that had been rented out to a hardworking crofter who had cleared the land and dug ditches and made fields. He had built a sauna and a barn and a shed by the lake for keeping his fishing gear in. His little cottage had been pulled down to build a proper house for the young couple.

Everything else around our farm bore his axe marks in the timbers. When we sat in the sauna we saw the faint outline of the crofter's initials above the tiny window.

'Was he angry about leaving?' I asked Grandmother.

There was a long silence. Then Grandmother said who could tell, but that he was probably a communist anyway.

So Grandfather and Grandmother had come to live on the crofter's land. After a few years they were given three more fields that Grandfather said he would measure the way he had been taught in agricultural college. With much huffing and puffing, and with paper and pen and strings and poles, he set to.

Grandmother said he should harness the horse and plough a field instead and get the potatoes into the ground. But no. Grandfather said that yes, he had noticed that they had five children to feed, but he was no mere brute or farm-hand. He had a bit of knowledge between his ears and he was going to use it. So even though the weather was rotten and the rain started coming down heavy he went out to walk his new land.

And so it came about that his agricultural college trai killed him. He got drenched to the skin and he was cursing. And then he had to do it again because he arrived at an impossible figure the first time. Poor Grandfather.

Did Grandmother heat the sauna while he was out? Did she have dry clothes ready for him and hot coffee? And a warm bed?

I don't think so, because he came down with pneumonia and died. Just like that, a chill, a little cough, a temperature and he was gone. He made death look so easy and effortless – and that is the true artistry, of course. To make it look easy.

But he was only thirty-eight, and he left Grandmother a widow with five children on an Iron Age farm.

The bastard.

5

FATHER SAID WE MUST OBEY INSTANTLY. Not try and figure things out for ourselves. He had seen for himself how dangerous that could be. When he was a teenager in the trenches the fat boy next to Father stuck his head out over the top and got a Russian bullet through the skull. Even though the officer had ordered 'Down'.

Another lad refused to run out of the trench when the order came to attack. He was shot by a Finnish bullet later, after a short court martial. That's how lethal not obeying orders was.

We did not believe him so we were always in trouble. The bundle of birch was over the door to remind us to obey, but we forgot.

Tapio and Tuomas, my older brothers, were hardened smokers by six and seven, although Father had forbidden them to smoke and beat them with the birch every time he smelled smoke on their breath. They smoked butts of cigarettes that they found on the way home from school.

The butts made them nauseous and dizzy. And the birch hurt their backs and Father's rage frightened the wits out of them.

Still they smoked. It was their destiny to become men, and all men smoked. Like Spartan boys they took punishment as their fate.

Father said he was at a loss on how to instill manly values in the boys now that the Civil Guard had been disbanded. He himself had learnt manly values there, such as never let pain and suffering show in your face. Just march on and let the blisters bleed into your boots. Never complain. Bear up. Be a man. Tapio and Tuomas heard what he said and had taken the matter in hand themselves.

I wanted very much to be good, but my craving for butter was stronger. Stronger than my fear of Father in a roaring rage: 'The girl has her blasted fingers in the butter dish again!'

It was my fingers that did it. I could not really help it. Somehow my fingers always ended up in the butter dish. I could only look on as those pudgy fingers got coated in tasty yellow butter.

I got smarter over time. I started asking Mother for a slice of bread and butter when the craving came over me. Usually she gave it to me. I would run out and lick the butter off the bread. The slice of bread I would hide under a bush.

S.K.T

This was bad. It showed disrespect for our daily bread that came straight from our Father in heaven. And I had thrown it on the ground in under a bush! It could hardly get worse than that. Even giving it to the pig would have been better. I felt afraid and waited for something to happen.

Nothing happened so I went in and asked Mother for another slice.

BUT MY UNDERHAND WAYS and slyness did not always help. There were also the punishable accidents over which I had no control. Things slipped through my buttery fingers and broke. I fell over and cried. I talked when I should have been quiet. I stood in the way of grown-ups when they carried heavy things. And so on. I did everything that a good child should not do.

It must have been a Sunday when the worst happened. I think so because there was a white tablecloth out on the big table in the main room. Father was writing something. His pen was rasping over the white paper. The inkwell was at his elbow. I loved to draw, especially houses with the gable end and front with all the windows and the front door and chimney. I could have drawn them in my sleep, I was that good. I pushed my head in under Father's arm to take a closer look at what he was doing.

First there was the enormous whiteness of the tablecloth. Then the splash of the inkwell and then the puddle of ink spreading fast over that whiteness. One minute white, then inky black and spreading. White, then black.

Father exploded like a hand grenade hitting a rock. He grabbed me by the arm and threw me across the room. When I landed, his practiced arm was swinging the birch over me like a windmill in a storm. The curses came in a stream of staccato Finnish, '*voi saatanan peRRR-ke-LEH*!!!'

Mother's face was white at the other side of the room, her mouth like a thin line cut with a sharp knife.

Then it was over. I was winded from roaring. Father picked me up and asked was I Daddy's girl. I had the gulps now and I could not speak. Father said answer me but my mind was blank, my arms hung dead by my sides. I was black inside from the hatred. Father hugged me anyway and cooed 'You are a good little girl'.

He was in a good mood.

Mother put me to bed then.

'It's the war,' she said, 'Father's nerves are shot.' It was from all the bad things he had seen and been through. In Karelia, the Russians had speared little children like me. Could I imagine that? Speared through their backsides up through their mouths and left to dry in the cold air. Could I not see that we were better off with Father rather than the Russians?

It took me a long time to go asleep. I listened to the rustling of the insects we called *russakka* in the moss between the timbers and the creaking of the house that sounded like groans.

Mother had given me something to think about.

6

THE SUN NEVER SET on our arctic idyll in the summer. The 'nightless nights' were bright and relentless. Those who were able for it worked all the hours God gave them to bring in the hay and the barley from the fields. I spent many hours on my own in the house, talking to myself and my rag doll, lying on the floor whispering stories into the dark cracks between floorboards. The buzzing of the flies and their soft hairy feet crawling across my face made me sleepy …

I woke when a shadow fell over me. I knew straight away something strange was about because of the smell. I looked up at the creature in black standing over me. She was as wide as she was tall. Her skirts went down all the way to the floor. She wore a black coat although it was in the middle of summer. She seemed to wear any amount of layers of clothes. She was scary! The smell was the worst. Rank, musty, mouldy, fishy.

I ran in behind the stone oven and peered out at her.

The creature parked herself on the bench by the door. She kept muttering and drooling. She was not leaving until she got coffee, she hissed. She was here for the day, so. Her bare feet were green because she walked in the grass beside the road to save on shoe leather, like all witches. She carried her boots on a string around her neck.

The dust sparkled around her in the sunlight. Or was it … electricity?

I stayed behind the stone oven and covered my eyes. She had been to our house before. Father said she was a witch – a *noita-akka*. He had once seen with his own eyes how she had rid a house of spooky noises. She had caught the noises in a leather purse and carried it down to the lake. She had said the magic words that would drown the noises and when the purse was thrown on the water it had sizzled and shot across before it sank. There were no noises in that house after that.

This was backwardness and superstition, Father said. He did not believe in this nonsense. He said best not to have anything to do with the witch. Sometimes it is best to forget what you have seen with your own eyes.

I closed my eyes for a long time hoping she would go away. Every time I stuck my head out from behind the stone oven I covered my face with my hands and peered out between my fingers. She was still there, but she seemed angrier every time I looked.

After what felt like a whole day she stood up and stamped her feet and muttered something incomprehensible and left, slamming the door.

When Grandmother came back from the field to start the midday meal for the harvesters, I told her. She sat down heavily. This is bad news, she said wiping her hands on her apron, bad news indeed.

7

AND BAD WAS INDEED TO FOLLOW. The next morning Mother came running in out of breath and upset. She said that our two cows had been hurt in the far field. She had gone to milk them and found they had broken the fence. They were in the next field that belonged to the neighbours. Each had a piece of skin ripped off from their flanks. A piece of skin the size of her palm.

Father choked on his coffee. He jumped to his feet with a curse and made across the room to take his rifle down. He ran towards the door roaring. Then he hesitated and put the rifle down by the door in the porch. He told Tuomas and Tapio not to go next or near it or he would give them such a hiding that they would not remember their first, middle or last name.

He ran out and Mother ran after him.

Grandmother sat down and we stood around her and asked her what now.

Tuomas and Tapio kept looking over at the rifle. We waited. Father came back and had a row with Grandmother. If he had the right tools that fence would have been mended long ago. Grandmother said that a useless man blames his tools.

We went behind the stove oven to hide and covered our ears.

Mother came back after milking and put the coffee on.

Father said that if the witch came back to try and nail those pieces of skin to the barn door, or to do some other trickery, she would get a bullet in the arse.

'But she is just a poor, unfortunate old woman,' Mother said. Father told her to stop talking because she knew nothing.

Father was always telling Mother to shut up. He had married her for her good looks and plucky attitude. Then he set to, trying his damndest to destroy both the looks and the attitude.

When Father was thirteen his own father had died and Father became the man of the house. But his mother, our Grandmother, was still his boss.

When Mother was thirteen she was the second eldest girl in a family of seven children. Her father was a shoemaker, and worked away from home for weeks on end.

He travelled to farms where a bundle of hides would be waiting and he would get to work, making shoes and boots for the farmer's household. All sizes, all made to measure. He was good at his craft and when there was work he was paid well enough to keep his family fed. And he never beat them and they were happy.

Then his wife, our mother's mother, caught the flu and died.

Without a wife, a travelling shoemaker could not keep his children. There had not been time to grieve because money was running out. So the little ones were given away to be fostered by farmers, who would keep them because it was their Christian duty. Also they would get a bit of work out of them in a year or two, for a relatively small investment.

And Mother and her sister Mariatta packed their rucksacks and went out to find work. And work there was plenty of in those days! Lots of work for strapping girls of thirteen and fourteen who could work hard seven days a week for a bowl of food and a few markka a month.

So Mother was alone in the world then. She was the master of her own fate but not in circumstances of her choosing.

Still, she was her own boss.

Father had been as far as Karelia with the army. Mother had only moved around Finland.

Father had travelled far on the guided package tour arranged by the Army with the bullets flying around his ears.

Mother had been the solo backpacker, a young girl alone in the world and nobody to tell her what to do. She got a shadow on her lung and was sent to a sanatorium far away. When she was cured she was sixteen and was offered a train ticket to wherever took her fancy.

They had both been brave but Father was not interested in the bravery of women.

'Not that you could call a woman brave anyway,' Father snorted.

A brave woman? It was against nature – like a bearded lady.

The witch often returned to our farm house. She would come in and sit on the bench by the door. Although she was not exactly welcome, Father did not give her a bullet in the backside either. If there was coffee in the pot Mother would give her a cup and in return she would get news of her relatives that the old woman knew.

Tapio and Tuomas and I always hid while she was in the house and Grandmother would go into the kitchen and close the door and stay there. She did not approve of Mother giving the witch coffee. Apart from the odd saw blade and axe head that Father needed, only coffee beans and sugar and lamp oil were bought with cash from the shop in the village. Grandmother bought the cheaper green beans and roasted them herself in the little oven in the range. It was a long process and soon every pauper in the parish would get wind of free coffee being handed out to allcomers, Grandmother muttered. Still it was best not to anger the witch.

Grandmother kept a secret supply of medicines that she bought from the pharmacist, though only very seldom. There were the camphor drops for minor ailments. Grandmother often gave me a drop on a sugar lump and said it would strengthen my heart. And then there were the 'powders' that came in tiny envelopes and were painkillers so strong that one farmer's wife had become addicted and was found sleeping it off in the pig-pen.

I wondered who would win if the witch and Grandmother were pitched against each other. Compared to Grandmother, who owned a farm, the witch seemed weak, but maybe her secret powers were stronger than Grandmother's potions and powders.

8

THE WOMEN ALWAYS spoke quietly amongst themselves. If they laughed the men would say they were cackling. Then the women would lower their voices again and fold their hands in their laps and sigh. And tell me to go away and play.

Men used fewer words but they were allowed to laugh out loud – at other men's jokes – if the joke was any good. A poor joke was commented on long after the event. The lack of judgement in telling a poor joke was a black mark against a man. Heads were shaken and there was muttering. And if the teller had laughed at his own joke, then God help the poor fool.

The men told each other stories from the war, stories that they had all heard before many times. They were all about the horror of it and the deaths and they would laugh out loud at a new twist, a new turn of phrase.

Father told the story about standing watch one freezing night after an unusually bloody day. He stood all night on a heap of twisted Russian corpses that had frozen solid.

'It would have been cosier without them,' he said. That last line was a new flourish. The men burst out laughing.

When they couldn't stop Father felt it was safe to join them. 'Ha ha ha!' he laughed. It was not a good sound.

Tuomas and Tapio said tell the story about the man with the guts spilling out. Or the one about the horse going mad. But the mood had changed, and the men did not want to talk any more. They just wanted to sit together and think and puff on their cigarettes.

'The state of those Vanyas at the beginning of the war,' somebody said after an endless silence, 'you would only take the cockade off a dead Russian's hat then. You would not touch the rest of their flea-ridden rags. Then they got the good American stuff … best of.'

'When the English declared war on us I knew we were going to hell …'

'At least we were at war with gentlemen!' It was a tired joke and nobody laughed.

'And now even the *Sakemanni*, the Germans, who started the whole bloody thing get American aid,' another man butted in, 'only the Finns have nothing coming to them, the whole world has forgotten us and we have no future.'

Then one of the men stood up and said that listening to

whinging made him tired so he was going home to sleep. There was no future, but there was tomorrow. He would come back and help with the hay in the morning.

The men left.

9

THEN SUMMER CAME to an end, as it must. The sun touched the tops of the pine trees. The rays shining in to our kitchen were long and bleak. We knew we were in for it. The clock ticked and we sat in the dusk listening to the radio but not too long because of the wear on the battery. Father lit the oil lamp for a bit but the blackness hung around the corners of the room. There was less to do on the farm and Father went north to work in the forest to earn money.

His letters home were long and homesick. The other lumberjacks were rough types from all over and he did not like them much. He wrote that he had stopped smoking to save money. And he did not drink with the other lumberjacks because he did not drink to cheer himself up like some sissy. When he drank, he drank to forget and that was too expensive. He saved every penny, he wrote, and he was wet and cold while we were sitting at home all snug.

'Yes, all snug on the home front,' Grandmother said under her breath. 'I will write him a letter and tell him to send money home urgently. Saving is all very well but we have hardly any coffee left and we are nearly out of sugar.'

Father wrote that all the best timber was marked to be sent to the Soviet Union, as part of the war reparation. It was loaded on trains to go east to the Vanyas, damn them to hell. There was no future for us, Father wrote.

One of the lumberjacks had a plan to go to Canada. He had a book for learning the language they spoke there and Father had borrowed it and was now learning English. *Koira* for example was 'dog' in English. It did not seem that hard to learn. Father thought he would have enough English by the end of the month if he learnt a bit every night. Then we should go to America or Canada. Or preferably New Zealand.

Grandmother said many from our parish had gone to America. And many had come back no better off and maybe they were the lucky ones. Because God only knew what had happened to the ones who were never seen or heard of again.

Mother said nothing. Her own grandfather was one of those who had disappeared in America.

'DOG', I said to cheer her up, 'dog, dog, dog!'

But she would not smile. Mother and Grandmother had to run the farm on their own while Father was away. Mother fed the animals and milked the cows but she could not harness the horse that was waiting in the stable for Father's return. So she had to carry bucket after bucket of water to the sauna for our weekly bath night instead of having it brought by horse in a big butt from a hole cut in the ice on the lake.

She wrote only one letter to Father while he was away. It said 'Hope you are well. We are all well here.' She said she couldn't think of anything else to write, he knew how it was anyway.

10

FATHER CAME BACK for Christmas laden with gifts. He had bought Mother a bag of white shop flour for baking buns. It was a luxury we got as a treat at the rich relatives' funerals or christenings. The wheat grown locally was greyish and poor, and the buns baked with it were not as nice. Father also brought a colourful hat with four corners from Lapland to show us what the Lapps wore. We all tried it on and laughed ourselves silly at the thought of anyone wearing something that ridiculous. He had bought candles and bunting of Finnish flags for the Christmas tree. You could get bunting with all the Scandinavian flags but the Finnish flag is good enough for us, Father said.

On Christmas Eve morning Father went out to cut a tree for us. He came home with an enormous tree and Grandmother asked why had he got one that size. Father looked as if he was about to lose his temper and barked at us to stand well back and stay quiet and not to touch anything while he dressed the tree.

Tuomas and Tapio and I stood by the wall and I held my breath as long as I could and then I breathed as quietly as I possibly could through my nose. Then I held my breath again. Then I breathed through my nose again, and so on, until Father seemed a little less likely to explode.

Father put the candles up and the Finnish flags. He was in his element and kept saying isn't this great. We nodded from across the room.

In the meantime Mother was heating the sauna. Without a sauna Christmas would not come because you had to be really clean for the big day.

After the sauna Father made Tapio and Tuomas roll in the snow until they cried to make hard little men out of them.

On the way back to the house they rubbed my face with snow but they stopped before I cried, so I promised not to tell.

And then we were ready for Santa who would come after dark. We sat red-faced and well scrubbed in our good clothes waiting for him. The day that used to go in a blink of an eye dragged on and on.

When darkness finally fell (which it did in early afternoon), Father lit five candles in the tree. Any more and the whole thing could go up in flames.

The candles seemed fantastically bright, but the corners of the room felt darker than usual. Father said we must be very silent and listen out for Santa's sleigh bells. Tuomas, Tapio and I held our breath. Listening, listening, listening …

But it was Father who heard the sleigh bells first.

'There they are', he said, 'I better go out and hold the reindeers for Santa. He will be in a rush and will not have time to tie them up.'

After a while we too heard the sleigh bells just outside the house. We heard Santa stomp the snow off his boots in the porch and then he came in. He had a strange broad walk. He barked, 'Good evening all here.' He had a deep gruff voice. He had a big white beard that was long and matted like an uncut sheep's fleece.

His boots were much like Father's. His coat had the fleece on the outside instead of the inside like Father's and it was belted in with a rope.

'Are there any good children here?' he said in his scary voice. I was afraid to answer in case I said the wrong thing, in which case he would take down the birch from over the door.

'Are there any good children here!' he said again in a louder voice. He was beginning to sound angry.

'There are,' I whispered, I was afraid to look directly at Santa. I stared at his boots because they were the least strange part of him. He laughed his scary laugh from above.

Then Tuomas and Tapio each got a penknife and I got a pencil. I curtsied and Tuomas and Tapio bowed and clicked their heels. Then we got a bun each with sugar on top. I put it in the pocket of my pinafore.

'No,' Santa said, 'Eat it now, it's a treat.'

Then he went out and we could hear him leaving with the sleigh bells ringing. Father came in and we told him everything, the three of us, Tuomas, Tapio and me, sitting shoulder to shoulder on the bench munching our Christmas buns. We were as happy as the day was long.

There were bowls of rice porridge with cinnamon on the table but I was so overcome that I had to be carried to bed. I fell asleep with the bun between my teeth. It was the best Christmas ever.

11

THE WINTER CONTINUED bitterly cold.

Grandmother was going through my hair with the nit comb. She was giving out about the nits and all the other vermin that the men had brought back in great numbers from the front.

There had been three wars in Grandmother's lifetime. They were the Civil War in 1918, the Winter War in 1939, and the Continuation War from 1940 to 1944. The men always returned much disimproved, in her view. That is, those who did return and their woes with them.

'Was it eight years ago,' she muttered, 'and we still haven't got them beaten back.'

'Would we be better off if the men hadn't come back?' I asked her. Grandmother said I must stop asking stupid questions all the time, I had her worn out with questions. Always these questions.

Mother was sitting by the stone oven dangling the baby's bottom over an old newspaper. Every nappy saved was a bonus. The well was frozen and she had to bring snow inside in buckets and melt it on the range. And then the dirty water had to be carried out.

She looked tired and there would be no point asking her either.

I was counting my buttons.

'*Pappi, lukkari, talonpoika, kuppari, rikas, rakas, köyhä, varas, keppikerjäläinen.*' The rhyme told you whom you would marry – a pastor, a sexton, a farmer, a rich man, a darling man, a poor man, a thief or a beggar with a staff.

'A girl with straight brown hair like a horse will be lucky to marry anything at all,' Grandmother said pulling the comb till it hurt. 'A few fair curls never did a girl any harm.'

'I am marrying the pastor!' I said.

'You will marry a poor farmer,' Grandmother said, 'or if you are a good girl in school and don't ask questions all the time then you could become a kitchen garden advisor. Best job a woman can have, next after teacher. Then you will have your own money and you could buy your Grandmother a fine new dress.'

I liked the idea. I asked her what colour would she like and she said black, black is a good serviceable colour.

'I will buy you three new black dresses when I am a kitchen garden advisor!' I said looking into her dark brown eyes. Grandmother turned away and said that black was a colour for sorrow. Did I want to bring her nothing but sorrow?

I tried to figure that one out.

The dog was stretched out lifeless on the floor. I asked Mother why was it not moving, had Father killed it, but she turned her face away without answering.

The dog stood up and walked away.

Father had taken Tapio and Tuomas to see an aeroplane that was due to land on our lake. There was a notice and a picture of the plane in the local paper.

The pilot would give you a ride up in the air for a fee. Father said it must be a real wreck of a plane since it had not been confiscated by the Soviets after the war when weapons and equipment had to be handed over to the Russians.

Some men in the village had greased their rifles after the war and hidden them under barns and under blackcurrant bushes. Waiting for the day when the Russians would come back. There was even a machine gun with all the bits and pieces hidden. Ready if the day came.

Three months in prison was what you got for hiding your weapon but that is a short time really if you take the long view, the men said with a snigger. What a joke it was to go to prison for doing the right thing. Defending yourself, for heaven's sake!

But for some reason a Finnish fighter pilot had managed to keep his old plane. It was a mystery how he could have hidden a whole plane. Did he disguise it as a fertilizer spreader?

The pilot was going to land on the ice on our lake and people had marked a good spot where it was safe to land with branches from pine trees.

I wanted to go with them too but it was not for girls.

'A waste of time and money anyway,' Grandmother said.

Grandmother said she had seen three airplanes in the sky over our parish at the time when Tapio was born. The peace had already been signed and a Soviet plane had come across the border to help chase the Germans out.

The three planes had been buzzing in the sky right above Grandmother. Two German planes were attacking the Soviet plane. Right over Grandmother's head it happened. I could just see it. Grandmother shaking her fist below on her farm and the planes fighting like crows in the air.

In the end the Germans set fire to the Soviet plane's tail and it headed east towards Karelia in a plume of smoke. The Germans flew north up towards Lapland to wreak havoc there.

When Father came back with the boys they were all keyed up after the experience.

'We saw our farm from the air,' Tuomas said, 'and the smoke coming out of our chimney! And our house looked tiny!'

'The house *is* tiny!' Grandmother said with venom, because she was born on a big farm in a big house. But nothing could dampen Tuomas's spirits.

'In the future will we all have aeroplanes?' he asked Father.

'Not likely,' Father said, 'but one day we will have a proper road. And then if somebody gets seriously ill, we could be reached by an ambulance with a doctor, instead of having to take a very sick person by horse to the doctor in the village on the dirt tracks.'

‘Why would we do that,’ I asked Father, ‘it would take so long that the sick person would die anyway.’

‘Ha ha ha!’ Father laughed. He looked amused so I said it again. The sick person would die anyway, it would take so long.

Father told me to shut up or I would get a belt.

Father’s good mood had turned sour. He said he was sick of living on a farm that was barely out of the Iron Age.

‘The wheel has just about been invented here in this backwater,’ he said bitterly, turning to Grandmother. But Grandmother batted back the comment without looking at him.

‘We are not buying a cart with bouncy wheels! Aleksis has a cart with rubber tyres and he will take the churn to the creamery. He is passing us anyway and it is no skin off his back to take our churn too.’

Our horse pulled a sled both summer and winter. The roads were bad and the sled went over the cut fields and grass almost as easily as over the frozen snow. We had a cart with big iron-clad wheels but it rattled so much that the milk would have turned to butter before it got to the creamery.

‘Even the gypsies have better transport than we!’

There was nothing Grandmother could say to that except ‘ah, the gypsies …’

When the gypsies came by they had well-oiled light chaises painted in bright indecent colours, red even. And their horses were light and frisky with shining eyes. Not like our steady brown workhorse.

Last time they came it was early spring. Father was away and Mother came out to give directions. They seemed to be new to the area and unsure of how to get to the next big farm. Mother had to explain twice, even three times. Finally they left.

Mother would have liked to have her fortune told but she had nothing to give them.

When Father came back he saw the barn door open and the hay gone. There had not been much left anyway after a long winter. It was the last straw! What was Father to do? He took his rifle down, whipped the horse and took off after the gypsies.

He caught up with them at the rich relatives' farm where the gypsies had been given shelter for the night and the beds had already been made on the floor and the babies were asleep.

But Father told them all to get up and get out and be on their way. Nobody argued because he had mad eyes and a loaded rifle. So the gypsies loaded their chaises and cursed Father long and hard. He would not have a day's luck after this. And away they went.

Father fired a few barrels over their heads and more and worse curses were fired back at Father. Bad luck as long as you live, they roared.

Now Mother seemed to be thinking back on all this. She worried about the curses. 'You should not have taken your rifle with you that time,' she said out of the blue.

It was because she said that she got the belt instead of me. A hard blow across the face.

Nobody spoke. A purple bruise was spreading on Mother's face. We all stood still with our lips pressed together. Just the way Father liked it. Still he turned on his heel with a growl and walked out.

He banged the door after him.

12

WAS IT BECAUSE of the curses heaped on Father that nothing would succeed for him?

It was not for lack of trying anyway. Three years before I was born or thought of, he had tried to start a new life. After one of the many rows with Grandmother, he made a big move away from the farm with little Tapio and Mother, who was already expecting the next.

He went to work for a slaughterhouse in our nearest town Iisalmi, and he rented rooms in Sonkajärvi in the countryside outside town. The work was hard and bloody and gave him nightmares, but he was used to that.

The trouble really started when he had to go out and buy up animals from farmers. The rulebook said that half of each animal, meat and hide, had to go to the Soviet Union as part of the war reparations. The temptation to circumvent the rules was great and so were the risks. If an animal could be slaughtered outside the system it brought Father a few extra markka in his pocket from a very satisfied farmer.

And was it not almost his patriotic duty anyway?

But the State Police, the long loyal instrument of the Control Commission, kept sticking their little red noses into the slaughterhouse. 'Let them count heads and horns and hides until the cows come home,' Father said, and folded his bloody arms, 'they will be no wiser.'

Father was close to getting caught many times but he always slipped out of their grasp. Nothing could be proven against him. And anyway his conscience was as clear and white as the newly fallen snow outside the slaughterhouse.

But keeping one step ahead of the police was taking its toll. Father's nerves were suffering. If he were caught he would be sent to the Sukeva prison, where the regime was Spartan even by Finnish standards. It was a cost-effective prison built in the middle of a bog, where a few armed guard and starvation rations could control a great number of men. Not that there would be much chance of running away across a wet treacherous bog that stretched as long as the eye could see.

Mother was worried too because it would mean a long wait for Father and no money. She worried about little Tapio who was getting skinnier every day. She worried about the next baby coming any moment.

The next one was Tuomas. And he arrived, ready or not, the way a baby does with no regard for the circumstances. He was born in the rented room with a midwife present and Father outside in the kitchen. His job was to keep an eye on the cauldron of water that Mother had put on the boil. That kind of task got on his nerves, the pointless wait for God knows what.

Then came the shout from the midwife. 'Go get the doctor quick! The child is stuck with the cord around its neck!' Father jumped to his feet and ran.

The doctor was young and nervous. He threw the scissors into the cauldron and fished them out again and scalded his hand.

'More a hindrance than a help,' the midwife muttered and turned her back and got on with it.

Luckily Tuomas was a robust kind of creature. When the midwife and doctor got him disentangled from the cord he puffed out his chest and turned from blue to pink and pissed in the doctor's eye and roared like a bull.

13

SOMETIME AFTER TUOMAS'S first roar the little family returned to the farm. Not much was said. Mother was glad to be back and she worked twice as hard for Grandmother. Grandmother never said a good word to Mother to her face. But behind her back she said: 'That one is a good girl and a hard worker.'

'It is not her fault that her folks own no land,' she would say and sip her coffee from a saucer contentedly. She now had double rations again because Mother did not care for coffee.

But the deadlock between Grandmother and Father remained the same. The anger festered in the air. When I was born three years later that angry air was my first breath. That air was so thick with rage that it hurt. I learnt to hold my breath, to take only small sips of bitter air. I learnt to hold my hands over my ears not to hear the rage. I learnt to close my eyes not to see the beatings. I learnt to hide behind Grandmother or the huge stone oven. Because both the stone oven and Grandmother stood firm against Father, rant and roar as he might.

In the end it was Grandmother who broke the deadlock. Some way into a row Father told Grandmother what he would do if she did not SHUT UP right there and then. So she took her coat and left. She walked out. And she did not come back.

Father waited. There was a feeling of doom; Father was subdued, not himself. He paced the room talking to himself. He admitted that he had acted 'unwisely'. It was as close as he had ever been to admitting that he might have made a mistake. It frightened us more than anything. In the end he went to talk it through with his uncle on the farm on the other side of the lake where Grandmother had gone to stay.

Grandmother would not meet face-to-face but she had set out her terms. They were stark and they were not negotiable. Father was to leave the farm and this time he was not to come back. Grandmother would get him money to make this possible. Timber would be felled and sold. Cattle and sheep and furniture would be sold at auction. The money would compensate Father for any claim he had on the farm.

Father's younger brother Antti who was away doing his military service would take over when he came back. He had been born with a hernia that left him somewhat disabled, but he would do. Father's three sisters had left to work in Helsinki, Turku and Kuopio as soon as they had made their confirmation. But being girls they could not be considered for taking over the farm. They used to return in the summer months with their disappointments and unhappiness and they were barely able to help with the hay and the household.

'Can you talk to her?' Father pleaded with his uncle. But his uncle shook his head. 'There is no talking to her, she won't listen. Is it true you fired a volley over her head when she left?'

Father denied it. But the rumour was out. Many believed it, only a few did not.

14

AND THAT'S HOW Father had to leave a second time, now with a bigger brood of children. Mother and the baby and me were put on the train. Father went in the hired lorry from the village with Tuomas and Tapio, two cows and three piglets. Nille, the dog, was left behind on the farm as well as Tapio's pet crow.

Our journey took us towards the coast. Father had got himself a job at a sawmill by the river that floated the timber down from the forests inland. He had rented the downstairs of a house for us with a landlady living upstairs. She had a habit of meeting any tenant's complaints with a sigh and 'I should burn this shack down.' For we were not her only tenants. One of the rooms was let to long-distance lorry drivers who came and went.

Our arrival from the interior to this municipality in the west was a culture shock. We were simple country folk, we spoke differently, we twisted our vowels in a way the locals found strange and comic, we travelled with two cows and three piglets. And so on.

Tapio and Tuomas started school and the schoolmaster immediately pointed out the two new boys as figures of fun. They had to get busy with their fists from day one. Tuomas had the sturdy build of a fighter, Tapio had spindly arms but he had the courage to take on anyone on the schoolyard.

But in the schoolroom they could not defend themselves. The schoolmistress asked Toumas about 'Father's occupation'. This had to be entered in to the classroom ledger beside every child's name. Tuomas innocently answered 'Farmer'.

‘Farmer is it!? Farmer!? How many acres? And what does your “farming” father grow? To be a “farmer” you need land, isn’t that so! Correct me if I am wrong! Am I wrong, am I much mistaken? Huh! Go stand in the corner, boy!’

Tuomas spent a lot of time standing in the corner with his face to a window that had been painted over to stop children seeing out and getting distracted from their multiplications and Bible stories. Being an inquisitive boy, he started scraping at the paint with his nail to make a tiny hole so that he could peer out. Suddenly an almighty box over the ear made him see stars.

‘How dare you!! You are destroying school property!’ roared the schoolmistress.

Tuomas was sent to the Principal’s office clutching his ear, his head ringing from the blow, for a proper punishment. The principal sat under a portrait of Marshall Mannerheim. A few rifles hung as decorations on the wall.

‘Now listen up, boy …’

But it was even worse for Father. He had been an independent farmer, but now he had to join the proletariat. It was a journey from one social class to another and there was no welcoming committee at the end of it. His workmates at the sawmill did not care for the airs he put on. They were the proud men of Ostrobothnia, the cradle of Finnish fascism. They had believed in a Greater Finland that would stretch to Karelia and further. But they did not like men from other provinces or faraway places and especially not anyone coming from an eastern direction.

And the cows did not like the shed they had to live in and besides, Father had no food for them so they had to be sold and we had to buy milk. And one of the piglets died from the cold.

But at last we had electricity. The bare bulb hung from the ceiling, reminding us that our lives had changed utterly.

15

AND THEN IT WAS Christmas again. On a small farm, Christmas can be made magic even with small resources. Now that we belonged to the proletariat everything had to be bought with hard cash. Somehow the magic did not appear that year.

But one of the aunts had gone to work in Stockholm in Sweden and a parcel arrived from her for Christmas. Thrill! The boys got a huge lollipop each with a picture of the Crown Prince of Sweden. The little prince looked like a cherub with blond curly hair and he wore a tiny little parade uniform with gold braid. Good enough to eat he was. But the lollipops were kept for a week to be admired before Tuomas and Tapio were allowed to do that.

I got a little comb for combing my brown straight hair. I carefully replaced the comb in its little pocket after each use and put it away in a cupboard.

Then something catastrophic happened. The parents went to have coffee with the landlady upstairs. I put my well-combed head down and fell asleep fully clothed on the settle bed in the kitchen.

When I woke up I was no longer on the settle bed. I was in a snowdrift just outside. Father had thrown me out the window! The house was burning and Father was at the window inside throwing furniture out.

'Take her to the neighbour's house!' he roared to Tapio and Tuomas.

'She has no boots on,' they said.

'Run! Damn it! Get a move on!' And the boys pulled me up out of the snowdrift and dragged me along, one at each hand.

The fire had got a hold of the house now and we kept looking back. Father was still inside throwing things out the window.

'My comb!' I called out to him.

But I never saw that comb again.

My brothers pushed me in the door of the neighbour's house and shouted that they were going back to the fire. Mother had already arrived with the baby. She looked close to tears and was talking with the lady of the house about bedding arrangements.

I went up to the window and looked out at the burning house. The fire was burning briskly and the flames lit up the snow far and wide. A fire engine had arrived.

Or not quite arrived, because the road had not been cleared after the heavy snowfall and the fire engine got stuck in a ditch some five hundred metres away. I could see the firemen standing around smoking and warming their hands and flicking butts into the fire, while Tapio and Tuomas were running back and forth throwing snowballs into the flames.

What few belongings that had been rescued were lying around, and Tuomas and Tapio were soon holding their arms out while Father was loading them up with what was saved from the fire.

Tuomas arrived with an armful of clothes and came up and stood beside me at the window and looked out at the fire. He felt that the extraordinary situation demanded strong language and he repeated a few of Father's long curses calling down the devil and his helpers.

'*Voi saatanan perkelen helevetin saatanan paska*!'

Our host and benefactor looked horrified at such language out of the mouth of an eight-year-old child in their good, honest Christian household. Although exactly what kind of Christians they were I don't know. I noticed later that one of their children, a boy my age, ate raw onions as if they were apples. He peeled them and chewed big chunks out of them until the tears streamed out of his eyes.

But they were good enough Christians to have a family of six under their roof for two weeks while Father was looking for a new home for us.

Father carefully listed the belongings we had lost in the fire: a pair of scissors, two saucepans, a child's woolly jumper, a woman's underclothing etc., etc.

'It is for the insurance,' he explained.

The insurance company official came and held a long interview. The fact that the landlady had mentioned that she would not mind if the house burned down was noted. And she had invited her tenants upstairs for coffee and then gone downstairs to go to the privy? And the fire had started shortly after in a downstairs room? Was this not so? Father agreed this was true.

16

OUR NEW ABODE was in an abandoned fever hospital. Was it TB patients it had housed? The three small, unfurnished rooms were bitterly cold, but there was a range in one room and a tall stove in the other. Soon Mother had the fires burning and the rooms became bearable. The small anteroom could not be heated so it could only be used for storing our scorched belongings. Perhaps it had been the nurse's office for seeing the patients.

The main hospital ward, with a separate entrance, was also empty and we spent hours playing in the icy ward and looking at mysterious pieces of equipment and dark brown bottles with remnants of poison in them. There were information leaflets lying around with pictures that clearly showed the advantage of having blond hair in a fashionable style and rosy cheeks and a happy smiling face instead of lank hair, pale sunken cheeks, ragged clothes and a downcast expression.

Then a family moved in to the ward and we had to play outside.

When summer came our former landlady sued Father for slander but the case was thrown out of court. And the insurance company had mislaid Father's list, *voi saatanan helevetin* ...

Father bought an old motorbike, a BMW, and started riding up and down the country looking for a future for us. Sometimes he brought me along. I sat on the petrol tank holding on to the screw top with both hands and with my Father's arms on either side. We had the wind in our hair and I felt as snug as a bug in a storm. We called in to distant cousins here and there, girls who had left farms and found work in small towns in Ostrobothnia. After each trip Father had to hide the bike carefully in the woodshed because it was not insured.

After many trips Father said there clearly was no future within a motorbike ride of us.

He sold the bike and went to Sweden to see if there was a future there.

17

NOW MOTHER WAS left with four children and just enough money to feed us. And plenty of orders and instructions. Father would send more money when he found work.

Without Father around we didn't bother obeying Mother. I was now six and suited myself, nobody was to tell me what to do. And Tuomas and Tapio fought back in school all the time and Mother was called in to the teacher to be given out to. She came home and burnt the boys' comic books one by one in the range.

'Teacher says if you keep reading this rubbish you will never learn to read proper books.' The boys said bad words under their breath.

Letters kept coming from Sweden with small sums of money. Father wrote that he was homesick. He could not speak the language so he had nobody to talk to except other Finns. And Father did not want to talk to them as they were mostly bachelors and spent all they earned on drink on Saturday. Father lived on bread and margarine, as he did not know how to cook.

He had tried working at a big estate in Småland owned by

a mouldy-nosed old countess but it didn't work out. He had worked in the ironworks in Hagfors but the work was so heavy and dirty that he became ill after a month. It was piecemeal work and the pay was good if you worked hard. He got 800 krona after the month. Don't spend it all at once! He had found another job in a paper mill where all the heavy lifting was done by cranes. The work was fairly easy.

Mother read out bits of the letters to us. She cried all the time now for whatever reason. I began to miss Father because with him around at least we knew why Mother was crying. Hoping that Father would be home soon, I began to teach myself Swedish to impress him on his return. My method was simple; I made up strange words that sounded Swedish to me.

'*Hookus pookus hurrah mannerheim aprakatapra svinhufvud ruotsi …*' I could just see how amazed Father would be when he came back.

'Christ! The girl speaks fluent Swedish!' he would say.

18

AND HE DID come back. I woke up one morning and heard voices in the kitchen. Father had come back in the night! Mother was crying because Father had bought her a wristwatch from Sweden. I hid behind the door. Father seemed strange and suave in a way that people were when they had been far away.

The following week Mother packed our things and Father had some things sent over by freight and then we were all set to go on the train to Turku where we would all take the boat across to Sweden.

Or not quite all of us.

'Antti may never have a wife or a son so the farm will go to Tapio,' Father said, looking pleased with his calculations. Mother was clenching her hands and her mouth had that cut look.

'But …'

Father glared at her, which meant button up or else. But then he relented and said Tapio would have a say in it. So he asked Tapio whether he was a mouse or a man and then it was decided. He would be sent back to Grandmother just the way he wanted himself, good man.

'I am going with Tapio!' Tuomas cried, because he and Tapio were inseparable.

But Father said the matter was closed and he was losing patience with everyone having an opinion now.

We all shut up.

'Anyway, nobody has more than two children in Sweden. Four is a bit of a heap.'

So the next day Father took Tapio by the hand and led him to the railway station and put him on the train going east. Uncle Antti would meet him the other end, even though Tapio could find his own way, big boy that he was. But since he had a heavy bag to carry maybe it was best he was met, Father said magnanimously. He had telephoned the shop in the village and left a message for Antti.

The rest of us went on another train to Turku where we boarded the passenger ship MS Birger Jarl. Mother had never seen the sea and was nervous. She was clutching the baby and when the ship left the quay she shouted:

'We are for Sweden now! It is too late to change our minds!'

Father laughed his joyless laugh as we watched our homeland disappear in the dusk. Tuomas and I went off to explore the ship. Father had told us to find a bench to sleep on because we would not arrive in Stockholm until the following morning.

Mother had a berth in a cabin for herself and the baby.

Tuomas and I were not used to being together on our own. Tapio was his brother-in-arms and I was usually told to get lost or else. So I walked behind Tuomas and he pretended he did not know me. From behind he looked lonely and dejected without Tapio. We walked the ship in silence and looked at the big grey Baltic waves slapping the sides of the ship.

We saw our parents in the bar, looking out of place. Father told us to go away and find somewhere to sleep now.

When we found a long wooden bench in a warm spot indoors we rolled up our coats for pillows and settled down for the night.

And so we arrived the next morning in Sweden, a country that had been at peace for well over a hundred years, where nobody knew anyone who had been in a war, where people looked prosperous and healthy, where people seemed at ease with themselves and at peace with the world.

But we brought our war with us. The shrapnel that had gone into Father's legs, in 1944 in the painful retreat when the war was lost, had somehow worked its way into his children. Each one of us carried a shard of that iron in our hearts.

We would never be at peace. Not in Sweden. Not anywhere.

Part Two

1

AFTER A NIGHT crossing over the Baltic Sea we finally arrived in Stockholm. Tuomas and I stood on deck and watched the harbour crew tie the ship's ropes and shout to each other in their singsong Swedish. Father had our two suitcases lined up beside us and Mother was holding the baby who was crying into the cold morning air. 'Whaoo … whaoOOO … whaaoooo!' The baby was competing with the squawking seagulls.

The gangplank was finally laid in place and Father marched out, briskly leading us into our new country. He looked very smart in his new grey twill trousers tucked into high shiny boots and matching twill jacket, a fur-lined hat on his head. We were all well kitted out. Mother had a nice new coat. Tuomas had a new tweed suit with plus fours and a jacket. I had a new waisted yellow woollen coat with a velvet collar. Even the baby had a new coat but he had got sick over it during the crossing.

Everything we wore was new from the skin out because Father did not want us to look like some kind of failures. Even though we were because we were Finns and we had lost the war. Or was it Father who had lost the war? No, we all had. Even those of us who were born after the defeat.

Mother was afraid of the sea so the voyage had been an ordeal for her with the sick baby and all. But Tuomas was in his element and he had just told me that there were snakes in Sweden which made me hesitate to set foot in our new country. So I was dawdling on the gangplank until Father ordered Tuomas to hold my hand and keep me moving and not to lose me in the crowd. 'Move it! Onwards! Look lively!'

The other passengers were mostly men who had come to look for work. Some looked a bit worse for wear after a long night on the seas drinking, but on the whole they were all fit and good for many years' assembling Volvos and Swedish ball-and-roller bearings. Most of them would find work in the next few hours and be welding on a factory floor before the day was up. They would be welding and welding and saving up for months the way Father had, and then they would go back to Finland and bring their families over. Except the single men who would gang up in the prefabs that were put up especially for them. They would spend their money on drink and cigarettes. Because they did not have enough Swedish to get at the girls obviously, Father said with a sneer.

The few passengers who came from the upper deck cabins looked strangely glamorous. The men were freshly shaved and fedora-hatted and wearing town shoes and the women with their neat hair that had been in rollers overnight and handbags lightly carried in their elbow crease. Porters came to take their suitcases.

A rough-looking man came over to the dockers and seemed to ask them for something but they shook their heads. So he turned to Father and spoke in Finnish to him. 'Do you see those wimps! Never seen a war, those *mamma*'s boys.' And then he turned to Mother: 'You have a kind face, missus …'

He sounded like somebody from Tampere or thereabouts. Not like us.

'Don't talk to him!' Father warned her. 'Don't start gabbling in Finnish here, especially not with the likes of that one! I bet he spent his war in the Pine Cone Regiment before he slithered over here, the coward.'

We knew that the Pine Cone Regiment was those Finnish soldiers who had deserted and lived on their wits hidden in the forest during the war. Traitors, they were. Should be shot. Were shot if they were caught.

A dark-eyed smiling man selling balloons and toys had turned up on the quay. He pushed towards us and pointed at me and held out a toy monkey dangling on strings to Father. He smiled and made the puppet-monkey dance and do twirls. For a finale, the monkey took a bow to Father. Father seemed amused by it all. He slowly pulled his wallet out, opened it and handed a note to the man who held the monkey out to me.

I tried to hide behind Tuomas. But Father ordered me to step forward this minute and hold my hand out. The dark-eyed man placed the now lifeless monkey in my hand. It was soft and furry and about the same size as the rats Tuomas and Tapio caught in the traps they set in the barn when we still lived on the farm back home.

Father looked pleased with himself and beamed at me.

'Now play with it!' he said. I made an attempt to pull at the strings but I could not make the monkey dance the way the smiling man had done. Father turned away with a frown and put his wallet in his back pocket and said: 'We might as well walk to the train now that I have spent our taxi fair on a toy for the girl. It's not very far.' Mother turned to look at me crossly.

I bent my head in shame. I had always been a good child who ate little and gave them no trouble. Now I had cost them money. It was the monkey's fault. I hated the damn thing and its stupid grin. I looked at my new shoes and blinked hard so that Father would not see me crying because tears put him in a bad mood.

So Father picked up our two suitcases again and started walking. The rest of our belongings would come as freight in a few weeks. It was uphill from the harbour and Father pointed at the enormous building ahead.

'That's the Royal Castle where King Gustav Adolf lives with his Queen Louise. A bit of a beanpole she is, Louise Mountbatten, with a long face. She is English like his first queen. A king can only marry a lady with true blue blood. It's almost like it was back in our village where people sometimes married their second cousins to keep the land together. But royals marry their first cousins to keep their bloodline!' Father exclaimed.

Mother was shifting the baby from one hip to the other and sighed. But Father was warming to his story.

'But this Louise was not a cousin and a bit of a dark horse so the Swedish king had to send a messenger to the English to ask was she the real royal thing and the English replied that she was, as far as they were concerned and if she was good enough for the English she was good enough for Sweden.' Father snorted at this refined English snub to the Swedes.

'We could have been Gustav Adolf's subjects if the Swedes had not lost us to the Tsar a long time ago …'

'Can we go now?' Mother snapped. I wanted to know more about the king and queen and the pretty crown prince who also lived in that castle. But the baby was crying harder and we moved on.

I was looking up at the many windows in case the prince with the blond curly hair would happen to look out and I could wave at him. Maybe the prince would see me there and think wistfully 'that little Finnish girl could have been my subject.'

Father pointed to a yellow building beside the castle.

'That building used to be where the royals played ball games hundreds of years ago. But then it became the Finnish church. Still is.'

Mother said we should go there next Sunday.

I had noticed something about the people milling around. They looked different from us. It was their smart grey town coats, their smooth faces, the way they walked, the way they talked softly. And they stuck their noses in the air looking preoccupied. They seemed to lack any natural curiosity in things around them. They didn't look at us directly but then when they had passed us by some of them would turn around and stare at us and pass comment to their companion. I stared back at them. Stare, stare back.

Somehow my bright yellow coat that I had been proud of felt all wrong here. Or was it the monkey I was carrying?

Mother, who was usually full of chat, walked head down and kept silent.

Father seemed unaware of the glances and the whispered comments from the passers-by. He raised his arm to point with his open palm at the big granite building ahead.

'And that is the House of Parliament from where the Social Democrats rule Sweden!' He laughed out loud.

Mother looked at the massive building without saying anything.

I tried to dangle the monkey on the strings that now had become hopelessly entangled. When Father turned around I smiled widely and pretended to enjoy playing with it. I was wondering would I dare drop the hideous thing into the gutter and be rid of it. But I knew I was stuck with it whether I liked it or not.

We continued in single file, Father first, then Mother with the wailing baby, then Tuomas and me last.

Me and my monkey.

2

WE FINALLY ARRIVED at Stockholm Central Station. There had been grumbling in the ranks so Father had decided we would get the tram for the last bit. Now we were in the biggest building we had ever seen. Mother stared up at the ceiling and sighed 'Jesus!' Father just snorted because he had seen it all before. 'Pfff ..!'

We had an hour to wait for the train to the suburb where the paper factory was where Father had found work, and where our new home was to be. After wandering around aimlessly for a while Father said we should go to the café. He would order a coffee for Mother and himself and Tuomas and I would sit and not speak and be good.

When the coffees were ordered Mother started talking, because she had been silent too long and felt the pangs of not speaking her mind. This was not to Father's liking but he could not stop her.

After a while, a man sidled up to us and spoke in Finnish. He was of the type that Father called *fiksu*, that is, a man who dresses smartly.

'Ah, I see, new arrivals! I could not help hearing the old mother tongue. Let me introduce myself. I am a former pilot in the Finnish Air Force, twice decorated ...'

He continued chatting in a very amicable fashion about this and that. He assured Father that he had friends in high places. At the Swedish Court even. He said the King's son had been very well disposed to the brave Finnish people. He could arrange an introduction to a few people who would be good to know ...

Father's eyes narrowed. He had spent four years in the trenches mixing with all sorts and he had met a few shysters and card sharks. He had been under the wing of a released murderer who had got out of prison to serve at the front line. A civilian murderer that is, because at the end of the war they were all killers, of course. The murderer had taught Father a thing or two about the world.

Like when a gang of card sharks invite you to play a hand of poker for high stakes they let you win the first hand. This draws you in, and you won't stop until you have lost your month's pay. The murderer told him to pretend to be a simple lad, or just be himself, and start playing. And pull out after the first win and never play again! See! Who's laughing now! Father was no village idiot. He could read another Finn like an open book. It was the inscrutable Swedes he never learnt to figure out.

When the so-called pilot started admiring Mother's good looks, Father said curtly that we had to go and catch our train.

3

THE JOURNEY ON THE TRAIN to the paper mill where Father worked was a little fraught. Mother started singing a lullaby to amuse the baby and then she had turned to Father and asked him something and he told her to shut up. Could she not see that people were looking at her because she was making a show of herself speaking Finnish and letting everyone know we were foreigners here? She was to sit still and lower her voice. So she sat mute, looking crossly out the window.

But it was not she who had drawn attention to our little group. People were looking at Father's knee-high shiny black boots with his trousers tucked in.

We sat without speaking through the rest of the journey, allowing ourselves to be inspected.

When we finally got off the train and started our walk towards our new home, Father pointed out the sights. There was the great big house where the managing director of the mill lived, there was a fountain in front of it that was never turned on, and over there were the villas for the engineers and over there the houses for the workers' families. And in the middle of it all there was the factory itself with '1798' on the wall, for the year it was opened.

'The paper we make in there is not any old pulp for printing rubbish newspapers that people wipe their arses on,' Father said. 'In there we make the paper that money is printed on and it is made out of linen, not trees. Are you listening at all?'

We nodded.

Finally we reached the house where we were to live. Every house had flats for three families. The flat we had been allocated had two rooms and a kitchen and hardly any furniture. Mother looked at the two single beds and no tables or chairs or curtains. Father had not had time to organize anything more, and anyway he said he had wanted to wait until Mother was there.

'We will buy what we need next week and our bits and pieces will come by freight any day now,' Father said. 'Don't worry, and look, there is an indoor tap!'

Mother raised her eyes to heaven. As if she had never seen an indoor tap! But since we had not had running water in our last home she stepped forward and turned the tap on and off without saying anything. Just looking around at the bareness of it all. And then she turned the tap on and off some more.

Father turned around and told Tuomas and me to go out and play because he had to have a word with Mother.

'Where are we to go?'

'Out!'

So we went outside onto the porch. Tuomas seated himself on the top step. He positioned himself in the wide legged confident stance of a big farmer back home. He was fumbling in his pocket for a cigarette but changed his mind and placed his elbows on his knees and tilted his head thoughtfully.

Three girls his own age were looking at him some distance away. When they saw that he was observing them they started giggling and whispering among themselves. After a while they moved forward and giggled some more and elbowed each other in their sides and after some lengthy whispering and some more pushing they started singing, very tunefully I thought;

'Oh where have you been
Oh Billy Boy
Oh where have you been
Charming Billy …'

After the first verse they fell silent and then they turned on their heels and ran away shrieking with laughter.

'What was that?' I asked Tuomas.

He turned around to me with a big grin on his face.

'Girls!' he said, 'Swedish girls.'

WE WENT BACK INSIDE. Father said he had a treat for us. He took out a packet of ready-mix for sponge cake. 'With this you just add water and you get a batter for baking a sponge cake,' he explained. But since he didn't know anything about baking and he had never bothered to light the range for long enough to get the oven up to temperature he had just eaten the batter. It was rather tasty, he explained.

We watched him make the batter and whisk it with a fork. We sat on the edge of one of the single beds and soon we had a bowl of batter each in our laps. He handed us a spoon each.

We had been allowed to lick the spoon back home. Here in our new country we were eating it from a bowl. Mother looked dubious but what did she know about anything anyway. We were now in what Father called 'The Future'. It tasted good.

4

THE SWEDES TOOK TO US, especially the baby. They called him 'the pretty Finnish boy' and patted him on the head. Mother smiled and smiled. Then they turned to me but my unsmiling face stayed their hand. And Tuomas of course was a big lump of a boy. No pats on the head for either of us.

The Swedes had been good to Finnish children during the war. They had rescued 70,000 children from Finnish cities that were under constant bombardment from the air and where food was scarce. There had been talk of Red Cross parcels being sent to the hungry children but it became politically impossible for neutral Sweden to help a country at war. The only way out was to move the children and let them eat in Sweden.

So they were sent on trains from all over Finland to the harbour in Turku, where they were labelled with their name on a tag around their neck. And so on to the boat across the Baltic. And then on arrival in Stockholm they were met by a medical team who examined them and got them deloused. And if only they could have relieved them of their strange language with the harsh Finnish sounds that grated so on their benefactors' ears, they would have done that too. But alas, that was to be a drawn-out process and more painful.

Then the children were loaded on to trains to be distributed to foster families all over Sweden. At every station the children got out of the train onto the platform to be selected by couples who were willing to take in a foster child. The three-year-old blonde girls with curly hair were picked first. Then the small boys with flaxen hair. Then the slightly older girls with tight plaits and cross faces. Then the plain ones with snotty noses. Then the ones who were both plain and snotty-nosed and bawling their heads off.

All day the train travelled with its cargo of boys and girls, until the very last 12-year old boy that nobody had picked stepped out on a platform far from Stockholm where a couple was waiting. They had no choice but to take him home because he was the last one, the only child left on the train.

They must have taken him by the hand and led him home with no words exchanged between them because the boy spoke only Finnish. Did they feel the warm glow that a benefactor feels doing the right thing? How did they cope month after month with no common language? Did it get better over time or worse? I suppose every child had their own story. Mostly they settled in well and learnt to speak Swedish and forgot their mothers in Finland and the language they used to speak. And they started to call their Swedish foster parents *mamma* and *pappa*. And then after a long, long time they had to go back to their mother in Finland that they used to call *äiti*.

But by then they had forgotten their first mother and what they used to call her, and called her nothing.

Our new neighbours certainly felt good seeing little Finnish children again and remembering how good the Swedish people had been to the likes of us. And we reaped the benefit of this goodwill. Wherever we went we were observed with satisfaction.

At least to begin with.

WHEN THE FIRST SNOW FELL, the kindly man next door beckoned me to come to his woodshed. I kept well back in case he wanted to kill me with an axe in there. But there was no sign of that. He lifted out a sleigh and gestured that it was mine now. It was a fancier sled than the homemade one I had in Finland. This one had a steering wheel and iron runners.

When Tuomas and I brought it home to show Father he told us to bring it back to the man because we were not charity cases, we paid our way. We did not want something for nothing. But I did, I did! I wanted this sleigh more than anything. And even if we had wanted to obey Father we would not have known what to say to the man. So we took the sleigh away down the road and rode down the slope on the icy road. The speed of it was exhilarating, so we did it again and again while we tried to figure out how we could keep the sleigh.

We went back home and I told Father that the man did not want the sleigh back because his children had died and did not need it any more. Tuomas held well back because he was a big boy and big boys were not supposed to tell lies. I could see that Father was unsure of what to do. He clearly did not want to go and discuss it with the man with the aid of the dictionary that he carried in his back pocket. He was the only one of us who could communicate with the Swedes. But it was one painful word at a time while he flicked through his dictionary. Father cleared his throat and looked hard at me. I waited. He said nothing.

He was going to let it go.

5

WE WERE NOW what Mother called *ummikko*. We were people who could only speak our own language and we could not understand the language around us. And the people around us could not understand us. It was a terrible fate to be *ummikko*. It was like being deaf and dumb Mother said. Outside our own home we were like cows that could only stand and stare. The thought of being like a cow made her weep. We could only speak Finnish to each other within our own four walls. But this was about to change.

It all happened because of the letter from Tuomas's teacher. Tuomas had been in trouble at school from the first day. He was due to start in fourth class in the autumn but because he didn't speak Swedish he was put back into third class. He was big for his age and restless. The other boys taunted him and pulled faces at him, so every so often he would get up and pretend that he wanted to sharpen his pencil in the big sharpener at the teacher's desk. On his way there he would distribute punches at the other boys to wipe the smirk off their stupid faces. During the breaks and after last class the boys would gang up and get their revenge.

The teacher could not help noticing that the atmosphere in the classroom had got more restless after the arrival of the Finnish boy. And his face was bruised after every break and his nose was bleeding. He was clearly a troublemaker and something had to be done about him.

Teacher said that Tuomas was to leave last class five minutes before the other boys. This would give him a head start and he would be well on the way home before the other boys got out and thus there would be no more fighting.

As for the language problem, the teacher had a plan. The teacher sent a letter home with Tuomas to tell his parents what to do.

Father was mulling over the letter from school and flicking the pages of his dictionary back and forth. In the end he got the gist of it and he told us what the letter said. Tuomas was to learn Swedish fast. It would help if he made more of an effort to forget Finnish so he must not speak it at all. Not at home or anywhere. He was to use only Swedish. If addressed in Finnish by his parents he was to answer in Swedish as best as he could. It was for his own good and he would do better at school if he complied.

'That is ridiculous!' Mother said.

'Are we to go against the teacher?!' Father exclaimed crossly.

And so it came about that Mother and Tuomas and I spoke our mother tongue freely amongst ourselves only when Father was at work. Our mother tongue was a Finnish dialect that was quite different from the written language or the way people spoke in Helsinki. We twisted vowels into diphthongs, we ironed out diphthongs into long flat vowels, we added vowels between consonants, we cut out endings, we doubled up consonants inside words. All this gave a comfortable homely delivery to sentences, like the humming of a bumble bee with a bit of a cough. When we eventually made contact with other Finns who spoke proper Finnish they smiled behind their hand and said we spoke with a 'crooked jaw'. In turn I found their oily speech unpleasant and pretentious.

When Father came home from work he was usually tired and in a bad mood. He would tell Mother to stop gabbling to us in her ignorant Finnish dialect. We would never learn Swedish the way she prattled on.

He told Tuomas and me to go outside and play with the Swedish children in the snow so that he could sit down in peace and give out to Mother about all that was wrong in the world and the daily insults that he had to suffer. Much in our new country was not to his liking. He had to join the union in the factory and came home and showed us his union membership book that had been pressed on him and that he had to pay a membership fee for.

'Look at the colour of it! It's red!' he said indignantly, 'and once you are in the union you are affiliated to the Social Democrats! I'm practically a socialist now!'

Father laughed bitterly. He did not like socialists because they were almost like communists. He had once been a farmer, and farmers held on to the fields that belonged to them. Fields that communists wanted to take, same as socialists but the latter were more underhand about it.

Tuomas and I had built a mighty snow fortress outside and Tuomas told me to make snowballs with my bare hands because that made the snow melt a bit and when the snowballs froze they would be hard and icy. When I complained of the cold he said we could expect an attack so we should be prepared and have lots of ammunition. I should stop being a baby or he would throw me out of our fortress. So I continued making snowballs warming my hands under my coat in my armpits every so often to get the right hardness to our ammunition.

We waited a good while, but nobody turned up to fight us so Tuomas went back inside and left me to guard the fortress. I saw some children going on their sleighs down the hill near the factory sheds so I took our bobsleigh and ran out to watch them from a distance.

They ignored me but then one of them turned round and said in their pretty language '*Vad glor du på, jävla gloapa*!' I went home and asked Father what it meant. I said the words many times while he has searching the pages of his dictionary. But he could not find the words.

His dictionary often let him down. At work he was asked was he a *nasse*. He looked up *nasse* and wondered what they meant asking was he a piglet. Some kind of insult surely but he could not figure it out. Later he learnt that his high boots and jodhpur-like trousers, which was part of the outfit of a reasonably well-to-do farmer at home, had led the them to believe he was a Nazi. Clothes, like words out of context, could have different meanings.

But Tuomas said he knew the meaning of the sentence the children had shouted at me. It meant 'What are you looking at, ogle monkey?'

6

I WAS TOO YOUNG to start school, so every morning I went to the playschool that was open to all the workers' children at the paper mill. A kindergarten teacher was in charge of thirty children between three and six years of age. Each day started with assembly around an almanac. We were told what day it was, Monday, Tuesday, Wednesday, Thursday, Friday. A child would stand up and pull a leaf out of the almanac, and that was one day gone. It was to demonstrate that one day followed another. That time moved on. The four seasons were illustrated with a picture. Autumn was a picture of bare trees and leaves blowing in the wind and a man clutching his coat around him. There was autumn and winter and then spring. In summer there was no playschool and time stood still. Or maybe it was endless.

Then we did crafts. We cut out a picture of a bird from thin board with a handsaw and then we painted the bird that was a bullfinch. It took all of autumn to finish the bullfinch.

Then it was time for music. We got an instrument each. I always got the triangle, never the little banjo that I had my eye on. And then we marched around the function room and played our instruments and sang marching tunes. Or the other children sang. I never opened my mouth, I just banged my triangle. Ping, ping! Before, when we still were people with a language, I had been a six-year-old who knew a lot. I had been clever then and I could recite a list of twenty small birds when asked. But now that I could only make this one sound, *Ping!* I did not want to try and speak because it only came out wrong. Once in desperation I said one word in their language. I went up to the teacher and pulled at her sleeve and whispered '*toalett*'.

Once I knew where the toilet was there was no need to say anything else. Sometimes in the middle of her busy day the teacher found time to sit down with me and teach me words in Swedish. I would look into her eyes while she spoke to me and stroke her arm and hope that she would not stop.

Mother had heard that the teacher had kept a Finnish foster child during the war.

Sometimes I understood what the children were saying. Mostly I did not. I watched and did what they did. Towards the end of our structured day we had free play in the playhouse. The girls crammed into the miniature kitchen and fought over the pretend cooker and the little saucepans while the boys sat around the little table waiting for the meals we cooked out of thin air.

If there had been little armchairs and pretend pipes and newspapers they would have sat down there like little daddies after work. Mostly they got bored rattling the toy cutlery and eating pretend dinners, and left us to go build railways in the boys' area.

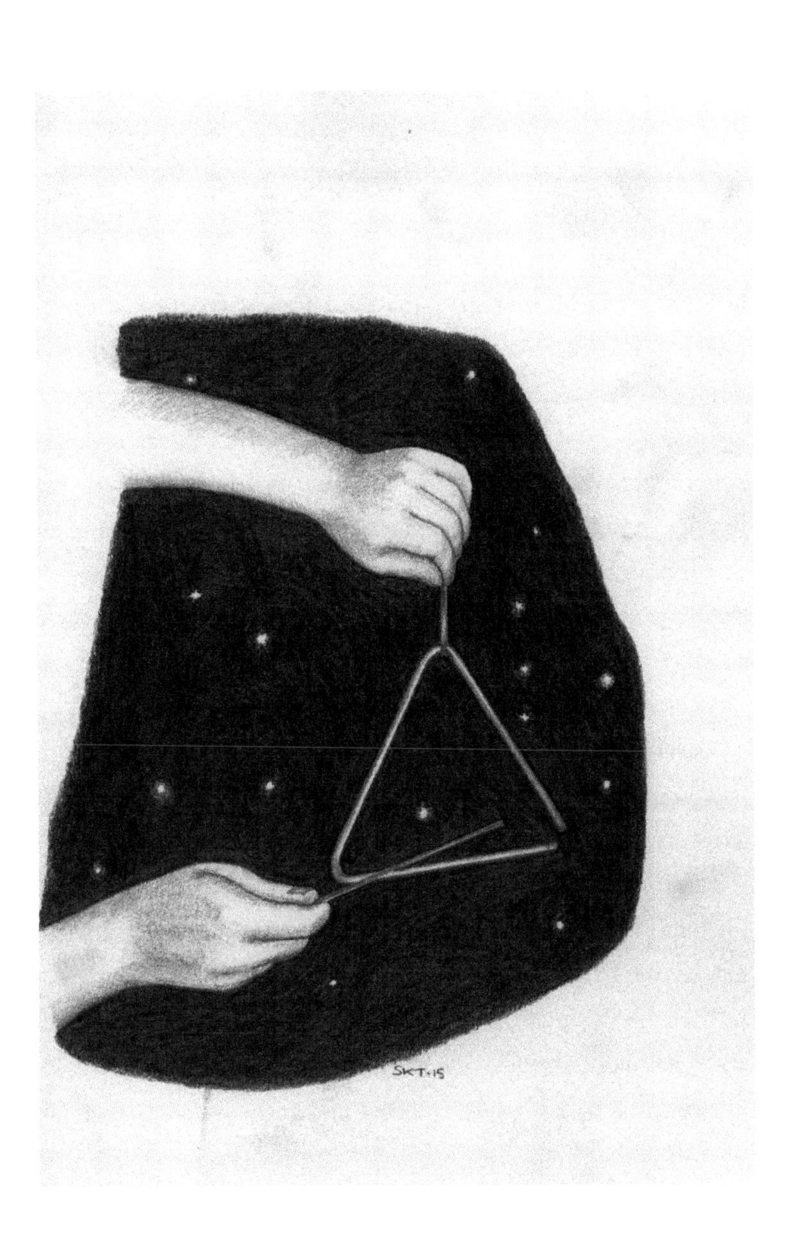
SKT-15

At home I did not speak to Mother any more. I had got into the habit of pointing and nodding in the playschool and Father did not like us speaking our language anyway. He preferred if he could have Mother to himself so that he could talk to her after a long frustrating shift at the paper mill. Conversation with his workmates was difficult anyway, but the factory was noisy and shouting over the din made it more so.

Some days Mother gave me Father's hot lunch in a metal box and said run over to the factory with your Father's dinner before it gets cold. So I would take off with the hot box pressed against my chest and at the factory the man at the gate would ring Father who would come down and bring me up in the big lift. The noise of the machine was deafening. Father would sit down and eat his lunch while I wandered around looking at the huge vats with bubbling grey stuff that was stirred by huge paddles until it was rolled out and became fine paper squeezed out between the giant rollers.

'Careful now, don't lean against the railings! If you fall in you will be paper!' Father roared over to me between mouthfuls while I wandered around being careful.

His workmate turned up. He waved and smiled and held out his hand for me to shake. Father pushed me forward. 'Not the bloody left hand!' he hissed into my ear.

Then he pushed me towards the lift. 'Go home, before you disgrace me further!'

I realized he had spoken to me in Finnish, the language he said we should not use in front of people. He had obviously thought the noise from the machines would drown out the sound and nobody but he and I would hear.

7

WHEN FATHER CAME HOME he threw his empty lunch box across the room. He told me to come forward because he was going to teach me the difference between left and right. He told me to put my two hands out and then he said that's your right hand and that's your left hand. Now put them behind your back. Now hold them out and tell me which is right and which is left. I did not know how he expected me to know the difference. My two hands looked the exactly the same to me so I took a wild guess and Father said that was very good. We did it again and again. Sometimes I got it right but more often I seemed to get it wrong. Father was losing his patience and started shouting at Mother. What was she rearing? A girl who didn't know left from right!? A girl who couldn't learn Swedish when she had the whole long day to learn.

That was when I stopped speaking altogether. I never said anything at playschool, but I now stopped speaking at home too. There was a strange safety in not saying anything. It was like being very small inside a very big bomb shelter and looking out through narrow slits that were my eyes. I realized I was safe inside, looking out at a very angry man. And I was not afraid. He was shouting but the words seemed strangely muffled and whatever language he was speaking (Finnish) had lost its meaning. Father was getting his belt out to hit me so I pulled my lids down and sat inside my newfound shelter in the darkness. It was all so funny and unfamiliar that I felt a little 'teehee' coming up, but I held it back. Best not to make a sound. I waited for the blow and wondered, quite calmly, would I feel anything. Then I heard Mother coming over.

'I think the girl has had enough now,' she said.

I STILL SPOKE TO TUOMAS, but less and less. He only allowed me to play in our snow castle if I made snowballs for him but I often abandoned the task and went over to watch the Swedish children. I stood some distance away and observed their games and they pretended I wasn't there or they would shout 'Hey, ogle-monkey!'

Sometimes if they were short of a player in whatever game they were playing, they let me join in and I would use the few words that were necessary for the game. Like *kull* was tags and *pax* was the sanctuary where you could not be tagged.

Mother continued speaking to us in the forbidden language when Father was at work. I had stopped answering her except in monosyllables. She would grab me and shake me hard and shout 'Talk to me!' But the shaking I got was like the way our house rumbled when the express trains passed in the night just fifty metres away. In the beginning we had all woken up in our beds when it happened and rubbed our eyes and felt startled. But after a while we did not even hear the trains. They came and they went. But Mother kept shaking me and telling me to speak. Then I said it.

'I want to go home! I don't want to be here, I want to go back and live with Grandmother and Tapio! I want to be where I can speak!'

I could see from the shocked expression on her face that I had said too much and I had made her sad. I wished I had stayed mute and not spoken.

8

FATHER WAS A THRIFTY MAN and he liked to hold on to his money. He had his wages from the factory and also his savings in the bank which was all the money he had got when we left the farm. Sometimes Mother said she would like this or that but Father said she would have us in the poor house if she was let loose with money. She would go on a crazy spending spree and then we would have nothing to live on. He told her she should try saving instead. Mother said she did not know what she was suppose to save when all the money she ever got in her hand was the money he gave her to buy food with.

'Well, you could buy margarine instead of butter,' Father said vaguely, 'anyway I have decided to buy a radio. Then we can listen to the presidential election in Finland.'

Mother sighed. She said she didn't care who the next president was in Finland because she would be in the kitchen spreading margarine on bread regardless of who was president.

Father went out anyway to get a radio from the radio shop. He was dressed up in his best gear because it was an important step to get a proper radio. And he paid in cash, no hire purchase for him because it was a despicable practice to get things that you could not pay for from a fat wallet.

And it was a fantastic apparatus he brought home with the names of cities around the world. When Father turned the dial you could hear all sorts of languages, French, German, Estonian, Russian ... But Father had bought the radio to listen to the presidential election in Finland. Father was tremendously excited when he plugged it in. There would be no worry about wearing out the battery he said. We could listen as long as we liked.

And we did. Once the radio was turned on it stayed on. I sat with him and marvelled at all the Finnish that came out of the radio. So many words in a language that I understood mostly. The election went on hour after hour and Father and I sat by the radio throughout it. Sometimes Father would jump up and shout and wave his fist in the air like people do at football matches. 'Kekkonen is in the lead!' he would shout. He was for Kekkonen. Paasikivi came in as a surprise candidate in the second round. Father marvelled at this and called out to Mother who was in the kitchen doing something and she came to the door and listened for a bit and then she sighed and said 'It's only men talking.' What did she mean? Did she think women could talk on the radio?! Father said that will be the day when we hear women talking on the radio, ha ha.

Mother asked me to come and help her peel potatoes but I shook my head and she went back to the kitchen. I was unable to leave the radio but hovered around it like a moth at a light bulb. Sometimes my attention wandered and I thought of leaving, but then I was pulled in again. The commentator spoke with the kind of manly timbre I found reassuring. How could there be so many words? How could he speak without stopping? The thought of women joining in seemed so strange and unlikely that I started to giggle very quietly. Father gave me strange look and said 'What are you laughing at, girl? What goes on in your head if anything at all!' I straightened my face. I said nothing. I was wondering if Tapio, whom we never mentioned any more, was listening to the presidential election in Finland just like we were in Sweden. But I was not going to ask. Everything was so much easier now that I had stopped speaking. I never had to worry about saying the wrong thing.

There was safety in silence.

SKT
SKT-15

9

THEN FINALLY SPRING CAME. The snow melted, and school and playschool closed for the summer. Tuomas cut willow whistles for him and me with his penknife and we played at being shepherds. He made bows and arrows and we played Robin Hood. He was Robin Hood and I was his merry man because I did not want to be Maid Marian.

Then one morning Father and Mother dressed in their going-in-to-town clothes. Mother was wearing her little brown hat and Father his newly purchased smart Homburg that he had dented just so. Mother said we had to be good and I must mind the baby and keep an eye on him and make sure he didn't climb the high stone wall and bring him to the toilet and wipe his backside, don't forget. Father said they would bring us a surprise when they returned some time in the afternoon.

How slowly time passes when you wait for a surprise. Tuomas and I could not really play our games because we had to include the baby who was fairly useless. We let him climb the high stone wall and told him to jump and we caught him except once when he tumbled over and grazed his nose. This added a bit of fear and excitement that helped pass the time. But the day was still endless.

Well into the afternoon we saw three well-spaced figures coming down the road from the railway station. The bigger ones on the outside were Mother and Father. But there was a little figure in the middle, walking between them like a captive. When they came nearer we could see that the little man had an expression that was both defiant and a little frightened. And he was clearly utterly exhausted.

Then we recognized him. It was Tapio! Our brother Tapio was back with us! He had travelled with an uncle on the night train from our village to Helsinki and then he had been put on the boat that took eighteen hours across the sea to Stockholm where Mother and Father met him.

WE WERE NOT A FAMILY that hugged and kissed, so we just stood nailed to the spot looking at each other. I was wondering if Tapio was the surprise or would we get sweets as well. Father carried Tapio's bag inside and then Tuomas said to Tapio 'Let's go and play!' and they ran off.

For the rest of the summer I was left out of my brothers' games and had to stand at the sideline and watch the Swedish children. The Swedish children asked me could I speak Swedish yet and I just shook my head because I could understand what they were saying now, and I knew lots of their words but I could not put the words together in their language.

They let me join them in their game of rounders anyway.

FATHER TOLD MOTHER that she had to economize, not be so wasteful with the house-keeping money he gave her now that there was an extra mouth to feed over the summer. 'Fill them up with porridge every morning,' he said, 'then they won't be hungry until dinnertime.'

So the next day, Mother made porridge and we got a big bowl of it each. There was to be no bread and butter until we had eaten at least a bowl each. I was not going to eat porridge! We sat around the table and stared into our bowls. Then Tuomas picked up his spoon and started to eat the porridge and the baby did the same, not knowing any better. But Tapio and I just sat and stared into our bowls until the porridge congealed and formed a skin and that was the point of no return when it was too late to change our minds. The tears were coming up in my eyes and Tapio too was blinking hard.

In the end Mother came up and said 'For Heaven's sake!' and cleared away the bowls of cold porridge and scraped it into the bin. Just in time too because Father was coming in the door after his night shift. He had a habit of snarling 'You are not in Granny Land now!' to Tapio. Or if it was me he was talking to he would put on a silly voice and say 'What would little madam like today? Half a peeled strawberry perhaps?' Tapio and I held our breaths. He asked had we been good children and eaten our porridge. I looked at Mother through the corner of my eye but she seemed preoccupied with something else so I nodded. I was a very good child who ate my porridge. Father did not like fussy eaters. When he was in the army he would have eaten a dead Russian's boot with the foot in it if it had been boiled long enough and served on a tin plate.

Mother had cleared away the plates. She turned around and said 'I have got a job!' Father seemed startled. 'You? A job?! How did you get a job?'

Mother said that she had got a job as a cleaner in the doctor's house up at the TB hospital. A Finnish nurse who worked in the hospital had come with her and translated. She was going to start next week. The pay was three krona an hour. Mother had said everything very fast as if she had rehearsed it. She paused and swallowed. 'And when I'm out the girl can mind the baby. It's only for a few hours.' She looked at me. 'Aren't you old enough to mind your little brother.' It was not a question. She had it all planned.

'But you don't know any Swedish!' Father said.

'Nor will I ever learn any being in the house alone all day!'

Father opened his mouth and closed it again and said nothing. Mother turned to the sink. She held her head down to hide a little triumphant smile. She was cutting slices of bread for us and spreading butter on.

She spread it on thick.

10

AT THE END OF SUMMER Tapio had to go back to Grandmother in Finland before school started. The journey back had to be planned carefully. Father had been writing to relatives in Finland. First Tapio was going on the night boat to Turku. He would be met by an aunt who would hopefully accompany him all the way back to our village. Or else he would be put on the train and the conductor would be asked to keep an eye out for him so that he would change trains at the right station. Father was in a soldierly mood and all brisk business.

'Chin up, you'll be fine! And you will get some sweets and a comic to pass the time, not to worry!' Tapio turned his face away and looked at nothing. His face was all bunched up and he was blinking hard.

Tuomas and I stood and looked when he left. It was like when he had arrived at the beginning of summer only in reverse. There was Mother and Father in their going-to-town clothes and Tapio in the middle being led away. We knew that he would have liked to stay with us. He had learnt some Swedish already because he was quick on the uptake. But what good did it do him? Father had decided that he was going back to stake out his claim on the farm, even though Tapio had no talent for farming and he could never get a horse to reverse in between the shafts and hated horses, which he said were the stupidest animal created.

When he returned to school the teacher welcomed him back with a 'Ah, we have our intrepid traveller back from far flung lands! How did you find the tight-arsed Swedes?' The Swedes had tried to do all they could to help poor little heroic Finland during the war and what they got in return was festering resentment and ingratitude, which is often the case in an unequal relationship.

Tapio was to do the same journey over the summer holidays for many years, until after some time after Grandmother had died when he came to stay with us permanently. Sometimes Father would travel all the way to collect Tapio from the farm or leave him back at the end of summer. He wanted to see the farm he had left behind. Also to show that he still took an interest. When he came home he would muse: 'They are growing hay on the far field now. Not what I would do. Oh well, the old woman is holding on to the farm for now but she will not live forever and my brother is never going to marry. He will want to keep Tapio on the farm and it will be his one day. That farm is ours.'

Father looked to the future, he said. He took the long view.

And then years later, one December day, things did go to Father's plan. Grandmother died on the farm exactly one week before her 62nd birthday. The doctor who was called out could only say that she was quite dead. He wrote on the death certificate that death had been caused by the frailty of age that had caused the heart to stop beating.

She was laid out in the outhouse where it was nice and cold to wait for the funeral that had to be delayed in wait for her children who had a long way to come. Tapio and Uncle Antti spent gloomy evenings waiting and listening to the groaning of the timbers in the house and the ticking clock. They missed Grandmother's wheezing breath in the kitchen and the way she slammed the pots angrily when cooking. Neither of them knew how to cook so they had no hot dinners. Between them the fourteen-year-old schoolboy and the twenty-six-year-old bachelor did not know how to boil an egg, Grandmother had seen to that. The neighbours' wives came by with loaves of bread and Uncle Antti would light the range and make coffee so, at least they had coffee and bread and butter and shop-bought sausage that they ate in silence.

A week later, Father and his sisters arrived and the sisters took charge of the cooking and Father walked the farm with Uncle Antti, pointing out things that should be done differently. He asked after the will, but Grandmother had left none, so things were to continue as before. Tapio asked Father could he come to Sweden now.

Father said no.

11

EVERY FRIDAY, Mother and I went to the communal bathhouse. Only the engineers had bathrooms with hot water in their villas. The workers' flats had no bathrooms so the mill had provided a bathhouse. It was open for the men and boys on Saturdays and for girls and women on Friday. You could hire a bathtub in a separate room for one *krona* but most people just used the communal facilities that only cost 25 öre. There was rows of showers, washbasins, little foot basins on the floor, and a sauna. Mostly children occupied the foot basins where we were lined up with the women's bottoms more or less at eye level. There were plump bottoms and skinny bottoms and the hanging leathery bottoms of the old women. There was a lot of laughter and camaraderie. Mother joined in by miming, and laughing when the others laughed. We always went home contented and rosy-cheeked after the sauna.

Father was sitting at home with Tuomas and the baby. He did not enjoy going to the men's sauna because it was not like in Finland where men sat and remembered the war together and patted themselves with fresh birch. His workmates talked mostly about football and their wages and the car they would buy when they had saved enough. Father did not join in of course, and there were incidents and confrontations over a bar of soap and such like. When one of the men bought a Volkswagen and boasted about it in the sauna, Father came home in a rage. 'Those shits who have never been in a war and have only one child at home can afford a car,' he said bitterly and ran his eyes over us. Too many children. If we were only one Father would have a car and he would be driving around with Mother in the front seat and one child in the back. That child would be Tapio because Tuomas and me and the baby would not exist. I wondered what it would be like not to exist. Maybe it would be much like not being able to say anything.

One Friday I was in bed, rosy and clean after bath night and listening to Mother and Father talking between themselves. Father said he would bring the girl (he never called me by my name) in to the school for a compulsory test before the term started. The test would decide if I belonged in a normal class or one for slow children.

'Why would she go into a class for slow children?' Mother said.

'Because she is dumb! She doesn't talk!' Father said crossly. But Mother said soothingly, 'Ah no, she is just very quiet. She is a good girl and she does not talk back.' When Father asked her when she last had heard a sensible word out of the girl, Mother could not recall. But it was not that long ago, she thought.

So the following week Father marched me to the school for the test that would decide whether I was able for first class or not. When we arrived Father did not know where to go. We walked around the corridors looking for the classroom and when we found the classroom all the children were sitting down at the desks with the tests in front of them. Father told me to pass the test and not to disgrace him and come straight home when it was over.

'Pick up your pens now,' the teacher said. 'You see the picture in front of you with the house with the big chimney and the flagpole? 'Now imagine there is a big wind blowing and there is smoke coming out of the chimney and there is a flag flying from the flagpost. Now draw some smoke and a flag!'

I drew the smoke and the flag blowing in the same direction as it was the only way that made sense. The next picture was a man without hands. The teacher wanted us to draw the hands coming out of the sleeves. It seemed a lot of unnecessary work to draw all the fingers so I drew a pair of mittens for the man's hands. I felt rather pleased with myself and twiddled my pencil and looked out the window while the other children were busy drawing lots of fingers. More fool them. And so it went on. All the pictures had something missing that had to be added. I had no idea why, it all seemed a bit babyish. When we were finished, the teacher collected the pictures and said we had all been very good and goodbye now and welcome back when the term begins.

The other children ran out babbling and they all seemed to have a parent waiting outside. I looked around for Father in case he had decided to stay, but there was no sign of him. So I wandered around the school. Every classroom had a blackboard and desks and a pump organ. As I was to find out later, every morning started with a classroom assembly with the teacher playing on the organ and singing a woeful hymn. Once a week there was a general assembly in the canteen with more talk of God the Father and his son Jesus and more hymns about God's creation, which was nature (spring and summer featured, and clear streams and sheep and shepherds). But that day I knew nothing about what was to come. I walked home wondering if it had been a mistake to draw mittens on the man.

A letter arrived some time later to say that I could start school and I would go into a normal class. Father was relieved. 'The books and pencils are free and you will get a big free school lunch every day. Make sure you eat up!'

So off I went to first day at school with a big new bow at the top of my head. I had a new schoolbag that Father had bought for me since the Social Democrats could not think of everything. Father had drawn a little cross on my hand with a biro. 'Go up to the teacher and hold out this hand with the cross on it, it is your right hand, and say what your name is.' He told me how to say it in Swedish and made me practice it and assured me I would get me off to a flying start. I would create a good impression which was important.

Again I was late because I was unsure of where to go. The children were already standing beside their desks waiting to be told to sit down when I came in. I went up to the teacher and held out my hand and told her my name. She took a step back and tilted her head and looked at me without offering her hand. I pulled my hand back and hid it behind my back. She smiled the way grown ups smile at somebody else's ugly baby and then she spoke.

'That is a strange name, we are not called names like that in Sweden.'

12

I DID NOT TELL Father that I had not got off to a flying start. He asked me how I had got on, had I introduced myself, had I shook hands the way he had taught me. I nodded. He was pleased with himself.

'I told you so, show a bit of initiative and you will be marked out as somebody to take notice of!' He went on talking about some time in the army when he had shown initiative. I stopped listening because I had heard the story many times. After Father died, Tapio and Tuomas and I tried to remember the stories about his life he had told us. But we could not remember any of them in full. All three of us admitted that we hadn't listened because we had heard it all before. We sat there a bit shame-faced, wondering how between us we could not put any of his stories together. How we could all have not listened.

Although Father said it was a good thing to take the initiative, he did not like Mother doing it and getting herself a job. Twice a week she was waiting for me when I came home from school with her coat on and said she had to leave to clean the doctor's house and I was to mind the baby. There was a new spring in her step when she hurried away, and when she returned with her pay in her pocket she was smiling.

Father said her pay wasn't much anyway and cleaning houses wasn't really a job. 'Well, it's a start,' she said defiantly. I asked her why the doctor's wife did not clean her own house and Mother said that a lady does not clean up after herself or her family and was it not just as well. Because it meant work for Mother and it was good anyway to get out of the house and see all the fine things in the doctor's house. And the work was not all that taxing and the doctor was a gentleman who always said thank you and goodbye and handed over her pay in an envelope. Mother said that one day she would get a full-time job at the hospital. Mother had become different. She saw opportunities all the time now, and talked about plans for the future.

I did not like the sound of that. Mother said she was talking about a few years from now. Maybe when the baby started school. The baby was her pet and the first baby she got to keep for herself. Not like my brothers and me that she had to hand over to Grandmother when we were three months old to be fed cow's milk out of a bottle while she was out milking and mucking dung in the cowshed.

Grandmother did not like children much and did not believe in mollycoddling. We did not know what cuddles were, and fought back if Mother attempted to hold us tight because we did not understand the language of affection. It was only the baby she had tamed who would sit placidly in her lap and spoke baby language to her with his head on her shoulder. Father would watch this Madonna with Child scene with distaste.

'How old is he now? Is he nearly four? Put him down before he loses the use of his legs!'

13

ONCE I HAD DECIDED I would never speak to the teacher I hoped she would not ask me anything. She mostly spoke to clever boys with old Norse names like Torbjörn and Ulf and Håkan. Not so much to boys named after American crooners and cowboys, boys called Jonny and Tommy and Benny. Girls with old names like Gunnel and Ylva were the teacher's pets.

On her rounds of the classroom she talked to me sometimes when it was my turn although I never answered her.

'Are you left-handed?' she asked. How should I know? Should I write with the other hand? She said it was alright to be left-handed. I moved the pencil to my other hand. How could one tell which hand was which? They both looked the same to me. 'Just write with the hand you are the happiest with! It's alright.' She moved on. But I was happy with either hand. It did not seem to matter. I moved the pencil back and forth trying to find the best hand. I could not tell the difference.

And then there were the letters that looked the same, like 'b' and 'd'. Teacher said think of one as a stick with a big belly and the other one with a big bum. But that did not help because it depended on which way they were going. I wasn't listening to her but I liked the sound of her. I kept looking at her mouth that she had painted red with lipstick. She wore a powder blue angora cardigan that I would have liked to touch but it was probably not allowed. I tried smiling at her, but it seemed to make her ill at ease and she asked what was it that I found so amusing. I stopped smiling and she walked away leaving a smell of nice soap behind.

The difficulty with left and right got resolved when we moved on from writing with our childish pencils and started writing with a nib and ink from an inkwell.

'Start writing from the window-side towards the wall,' Teacher said. It meant write from left to right which made sense, otherwise my hand smudged the wet ink. So the question was settled finally. I found the best hand for the task and it was the right hand. I found writing easy and spelling was not hard for me because I read so many books and the shape of the words stuck. I wrote essays that were read out in class sometimes.

'Well, what do you know,' Teacher said handing me back my copy book. 'Who would have thought you had so many words.' And I did, I was bursting with words, only I could not speak them.

In our first years in Sweden we had no books at home, apart from the Bible and later a phone book. I read the latter sometimes when I had run out of library books. I read the names and the addresses and wondered what kind of lives they had. People in the wealthy parts of Stockholm had several phone numbers, one for the man of the house and another one for the housekeeper and the children. This intrigued me and I spent hours making up stories about such families and their lives with two phones.

I had joined the library and had a lending card that allowed me to borrow as many books as I liked for three weeks at a time. I usually borrowed eighteen or twenty books, because I got greedy when I saw so many. I could have borrowed fewer and gone more often, but my shortcut went along an unlit path through a wood and I was terrified of the dark. It was the dark itself that scared me. There were bogeymen lurking in the dark of course, and dirty men with their trousers down and ghosts and wolves, but it was the dark itself that was the worst. I ran with my heavy bag all the way with my heart pounding while I tried to hold my breath so as not to attract danger. Every now and then I had to stop to breathe into my cupped hands to keep the noise down.

I read all of *Grimm's Fairy Tales* and all the tales by Hans Christian Andersen. Most of all I liked the story about the little mermaid. She had left her country under the sea where she was a princess and in her new place on dry land she could not speak because she had gone to a witch and traded in her tongue for legs, and every step hurt her feet like a knife going through the soles. This made sense, it explained it all. If you leave your true home you have to give something up. I had traded in my tongue too but I had got nothing for it.

I could not get enough of these fairy tales and stories where clever boys and princesses could outsmart stupid giants and witches. It confirmed what I had been guessing at, that you had to be a boy or a princess to get on in the world. I was hoping that, if I could not become a boy, I would at least not turn into a woman. Maybe I could dress as a boy and pass. Or maybe I was really a princess who had been swapped somehow with a peasant girl? It did not seem likely, but if you really, really want something maybe it could come true.

When I had read all the fairy tales I moved onto Astrid Lindgren and her books about Pippi Longstocking. Now there was a girl who made her own way in the world.

Then it was the *Famous Five* series, but the librarian removed everything by Enid Blyton from the shelves before I had a chance to read them all because they were 'rubbish literature' and bad for you. No amount of pleading could make her change her mind. Enid Blyton books would rot our brains, she kept saying.

When I had read everything on the children's shelves I moved on to Russian classics. They did not make a lot of sense. Why did Anna Karenina leave her nice husband Karenin? He had a good steady job in a government office, it was light work and he did not have to get his hands dirty and he could afford a nice house for the family to live in. He did not hit Anna or shout at her or anything like that when he came home from work but only sat there, silent and polite. So why did she leave the nice man Karenin and her home and her little son to go away with Count Vronsky? It was a stupid story and there were lots of boring bits that I had to skip.

'The girl is sitting hunched over a book again,' Father growled. Then he told a story of Grandmother's uncle, who had a big farm with lots of land and a house full of farmhands. Then he started to take an interest in books and joined the Young Finland literary movement and neglected his farm and read books all the time and the bank had called in his debts and he had lost his farm and his life was in ruins. All because of books. I had heard the story before. And anyway I did not have a farm to ruin. Like always when Father spoke, I kept my eyes on a spot on the floor and slowed my breath so as not to make a noise. And hoping, hoping that he would not go into a rage. Sometimes he switched to Swedish to lead by example. But he always lost his bearings in the Swedish words. He became hesitant, he said the words in the wrong order and kept searching for the right word and if he found the word it did not come out right. When I sneaked a glance at him his grey eyes seemed paler and greyer and uncertain. He was not very good at Swedish.

I remembered a story he had often told us about an officer who had a breakdown during the retreat at the end of the war. Father and his mates were running for their lives with the Russians after them. They ran into a lone officer who drew his handgun and pointed at them and shouted

'Stand to attention, you bloody deserters!'

Father said he and his mates stopped and put their hands up and said 'We are not deserters, we are Finnish soldiers, Sir'. And the officers sank down and sat on a tree stump and burst out crying and said 'Go on then, Finnish soldiers, run! Because this war is lost, boys.' And they did not know what to do so they left him there and ran.

I was wondering was Father having a breakdown. What would happen to us if he broke down?

I did not just read the books. I lived the stories in the books. When I was out wandering with the Swedish kids around the paper mill I was daydreaming I was in the Scottish highlands with Alan Breck Stewart from *Kidnapped*. I was his companion disguised as a boy, I was David Balfour. Only when I was mortally wounded by a bullet did he find out that I was not a boy. He wept and said that since I was a girl he would wait for me to be old enough to marry him if I lived and then we would be together always. Unfortunately I died in my story. I replayed the scene many times in my mind.

I got Mother to buy me a kilt that swung around my legs when I bravely marched ever onwards with my hero, Alan Breck Stewart.

After my death in *Kidnapped* I spent a long time comforting Robinson Crusoe on his island. I told him I knew he would be rescued, not to worry, I would help him. I showed him the knots I had learnt in the junior scouts and saved him from many tricky situations.

But most of the time I was the Little Mermaid in her beautiful underwater world with her sisters. I didn't care for the prince that she gave up her tongue for so I left that bit out. I took full advantage of my tail and did endless underwater backflips and swimming exercises.

The underwater world was more real to me than the world around me.

On Fridays I went to the junior girl scout meetings. We spent a lot of time drawing the Swedish flag to scale on squared paper and colouring in blue and yellow. Then we learned the rules for handling the flag with respect. Never let it touch the ground. Hoist it in the morning. Lower it in the evening. Fold it. Raise it at half mast if somebody died. And so on. I never really knew why we spent so much time with the flag. I knew that it was important because you had to know which way the flag blew in the wind to be allowed to go to school in a normal class. But only people who owned their own villa had a flag pole and their own flag that they flew when they celebrated their family birthdays. We didn't celebrate birthdays in our family and nobody at the mill owned their house. But in our schoolbooks everyone owned their own house and raised the flag on birthdays in their model world.

I was appointed leader of my patrol of junior scouts because I was tall, I had no leadership qualities whatsoever. And I never spoke except in monosyllables. One of my charges failed to salute our grown-up in charge correctly because I had not taught her well enough. When commanded 'Be obedient!' we were supposed to put two fingers to our forehead and answer with our motto 'I want to obey!' (This was before our motto became 'Be prepared' in the senior scouts.) The girl answered 'Okay' with both arms hanging by her sides. The grown-up tried to prompt her but the girl got more confused and kept answering 'Eh ... Okay? Okay!' She did not last in the scouting movement. Probably she never learnt any of the knots we practised through many winter evenings to little purpose. A reef knot will take you through an average life. Only the very desperate need a slip knot.

After the scout meeting I had to run home alone along the same shortcut that I took from the library, through the dark, scary wood. A girl from the paper mill had started in the scouts at the same time as me but left suddenly. We had to give parents' name and occupation to the grown-up in charge. And when the grown-up needed to know was my friend's mother 'Miss' or 'Mrs', my friend hesitated and said 'Miss' thinking that all women who did not have a living husband were 'Miss'. When her widowed mother heard of this and ordered her to go back to say her mother was a 'Mrs' the embarrassment was so deep that my friend never came back.

I would have liked to have left the scouts too, but Father said we Finns never leave our post or patrol but stick it out till the end come hell or high water. And besides he had already paid for my uniform. Father said we must blend in, be like Swedes. But we must keep our core Finnishness because Swedes were soft and had never had it tough. I couldn't make sense of Father's thinking. Did he want me to be soft like the Swedes on the outside and at the same time hard on the inside? Did he want me to blend in or not? Was I becoming soft all the way through like the Swedes because I wanted to leave the scouts and give up my uniform? It was all very confusing.

The school had a flagpole in the middle of the schoolyard where the caretaker hoisted the Swedish flag on special days. It had something to do with the King's birthday or some such royal event. We did not know much about the King except that he was very old and dignified and hidden away in his castle where he lived quietly with his queen.

One day, somebody had hoisted a pair of blue long johns up the flagpole. We noticed them but thought no more about it. The next lesson the principal announced on the classroom loudspeaker that all classes were to move out to the yard and to stand by the flagpole, each class in formation.

Like schoolchildren everywhere, we welcomed the break even though we expected a session of hymn singing and a speech by the religion teacher.

Once we were lined up in the yard and waiting with our teachers not knowing what to do except to order us to be quiet and stand to attention, the principal's car drove in to the yard. When it stopped a boy was hauled out by the scruff of the neck and marched up to the flagpole. It was Tuomas!

The principal shouted at him to take the long johns down and Tuomas swiftly undid the knots on the ropes, boy scout that he was, and lowered the long johns slowly. Perhaps unnecessarily slowly because the principal barked at him to get on with it. Finally the long johns were down and Tuomas started to fold them ceremoniously but the principal ripped them out of his hands and told Tuomas to get back into the car. Tuomas started walking, at first head down with his shoulders hunched, but after glancing around at the whole assembled school he straightened up and started his special John Wayne cowboy walk. He was smirking a little and winked at some friends. Even though nobody made a sound, it was as if there was a cheer rising from the crowd. The principal gave Tuomas a slap across the back of his head and he got into the principal's car in the back seat. The principal seated himself behind the wheel and drove off.

We stood quietly watching until our teachers started rustling us back in to the school.

'Disrespect of the Swedish flag is a very, very serious offence,' the teacher said when we got back to the classroom, 'Desecration of our national symbol is punished by … eh …'

Our teacher clearly did not know what the punishment was. Maybe the principal had taken Tuomas behind bicycle sheds and shot him? I was wondering how Tuomas had desecrated the Swedish flag when no flag had been handled. Were the blue underpants the same as the blue and yellow flag? Or was it the flagpole that had been desecrated?

The teacher thought about it and then he said there could be a fine or imprisonment or maybe a criminal record at the very least which would mean the offender would never get a job. And if the offender was a foreign national say, he could never get Swedish citizenship with a criminal record.

I put up my hand to say something to the teacher or maybe ask a question. But when Teacher asked me what I wanted my mouth opened and shut again, several times, like a fish on dry land or like a little mermaid. When the pretty prince spoke to the little mermaid she probably just opened and shut her mouth and only air came out. And she kept looking down at her bony knees where her scaly tail had once been. And she wanted to go back where she had been in her element but there was no way back of course.

I folded my hands in my lap while the teacher asked again did I have anything to say. I shook my head, I had nothing to say.

He said my brother must not think he would get away behaving like this. He said something about 'you people coming here and …' but I stopped listening and closed my eyes and wished I could sink through the floor down to the bottom of the sea where I would be the little mermaid swimming around in my underwater world. I would stay down there with my Father the Sea King and my Grandmother and my sisters in a palace made of coral with windows of clear amber, and there were fish swimming outside those windows like birds, and they were so tame you could pet them. And the King was a peaceful king who had never seen the war and the turmoil on the surface of the sea where storms tear cruelly at the water and fray men's nerves and make them so angry that they have to belt their children all the time or they will break. All is calm at the bottom of the sea, and grumpy Grandmothers live for three hundred years and when they die they turn to foam like all merfolk. And when we missed her we would go and look at the foam that floats on the waves because that was like going to a grave. Not like in Sweden where we had no graves to go to and the dead lie far away. Under the water everyone can stay together and nobody has to go away. No brother is left behind and there are lots of aunts and uncles and rich relatives to borrow butter from when you only have money for margarine. And you have a beautiful voice, more beautiful than any voice on land and you swim with your sisters all day singing with your long hair flowing behind you. Because everything is perfect under water. At the bottom of the sea one does not have to explain oneself all the time because merfolk understand each other and remember the same things.

I opened my eyes and saw that the teacher was standing at the blackboard and my hands were resting on my knees.

And I had no tail.